THE CUT N SHOOT CLASSIC

(By Invitation Only)

Stephen Banister

1988

ISBN

Hardcover: 978-1-969733-03-1
Paperback: 978-1-969733-02-4

This little book of none other than pure fiction is dedicated to the annual Hubbell Golf Classic and most everyone who has dared to participate. A special thanks to Larry, Mike and Bob for making it happen.

And to the wives, I again say it is none other than pure fiction. And you know golfers don't lie.

Give me golf clubs, fresh air and a beautiful
partner and you can keep my golf clubs and the
fresh air.

Jack Benny

TABLE OF CONTENTS

PRACTICE DON'T NECESSARILY MAKE PERFECT

And like my dear, departed daddy once told me. He said, "Son, somebody needs to take some of the character out of this here old game of golf and put some characters back in."

With those well-chosen words of wit and wisdom, I ended what had been my tenth annual war of words with a small army of local scribes. This year had been a little different from the rest. Station KHSN-Houston had graciously contracted to air our little golf tournament beginning with the just completed press conference and running two hours Saturday, and the same plus another half hour on Sunday.

Now folks, we ain't talking your Pat Summerall or your Lee Trevino throwing them pearls of golf wisdom out over the crowd high above the eighteenth green, but we did manage to lasso up none other than Billy Ray Breedlove, defensive end for the Houston Oilers, to handle the color, if you will. Old Number 99 just happens to be your better-than-average linkster, which is a hell of a lot more than can be said about his pigskin prowess. Not that I would say it without at least a four-hour head start. Billy Ray carries a 5 handicap, which is two more than the number of tackles he averaged each game last season.

Sharing the duties on the broadcast platform with Billy Ray, and yours truly had to agree

to this in writing before any further
negotiations could be made, is Channel 3's own
Bruce Conlee, Sports Director. Now don't take
old Joe Don here the wrong way. I like old
Brucie; hell, probably as much as I like a
strange fart in an elevator. Brucie is a nice
enough fella, as far as fellas go. I just
wouldn't want that prick seen with my sister.
Shit! I wouldn't even want him seen with my ex-
wife.

It ain't his ten-year-old, fresh off the
rack, polyester double-knit leisure suits or
his off-white, fake Justins so much as it is
his ability to talk faster than he can think.
I've heard more shit dribble out over his gums
than out of my own personal ass after a fifteen-
minute lunch at Lupe's Pit Stop and All-Night
Laundromat over Highway 105.

If old Billy Ray ain't fed Brucie his own
mike during the first hour on Saturday, me and
Thumper Boone are gonna demand he be traded to
Green Bay for a no better than undisclosed
rookie or tenth round draft choice, whichever
comes second. Hell, we've seen them Oilers make
worse deals over the years.

But what the hell. TV is TV and if them boys
can get their cameras up onto the Number 9 tee
box without considerable loss to life and limb,
not to mention expensive equipment, then more
power to 'em. It ain't but one hundred and
sixty feet of sheer straight up. Sort of makes
you wonder if a gaffer will bite when he hits
the green below.

Seems to me, I must have left my manners back
in the locker room with my Footjoys. My mama
didn't really raise no impolite son, so just

in case I ain't mentioned it yet, my name is Joe Don Buggs and I am the majority owner of the meanest little shit-eatinest golf course in all of Texas, and maybe all of Golfdom, should such a place exist outside the warped minds of those of us who would rather be beating the holy piss out of a little white ball than coveting our neighbor's wife.

If the Good Lord ever decided to give us mortals a glimpse of Hell in Heaven, all He would have to do is move that big old bright Star of Bethlehem right over the outskirts of Cut N Shoot, Texas. Course, he'd have to look elsewhere for some Wise Men, as they sure wouldn't be found on this course.

God and the rest of us can thank my daddy for this piece of work, although the revenge factor had a lot to do with it. You see, Daddy grew up in west Texas, Odessa proper, working night and day in the oil fields. He hadn't meant to get rich, just make a living and put beer in the fridge, but rich he got.

If I recall the story as it was told to me not more than a couple hundred times, he and his brother, Ted, won this little parcel of land over near the Capitan Mountain in an honest poker game one payday evening. I say honest, cause back then, anyone caught playing with one too many cards on their person was likely to have a widow for a wife.

Anyway, the two of them pooled what little resources they had, plus any others they could lay their hands on and drilled their first well, which came in as what you might call your garden variety gusher, and it was downhill from there. They parlayed that black beauty into thirty-seven more straight hits and before you could say Spindletop, they were rolling amongst the big boys in that big old oil town of Houston.

Now, old Leak Buggs, Daddy to me, seemed to forget where he came from or how he got to where he was and figured the oil elite should accept him as he presently stood. Big house in fashionable Plantation Oaks, two Lincolns and one Caddy, and Mama didn't even drive; and me, shit, I wasn't even a twinkle in his eye yet.

His rude awakening came about the same time that big old war in Europe was winding down to the final cut. The boys at Plantation Oaks Country Club planned the social event of the year to celebrate our eminent victory over Mr. Hitler. And like everything else that goes with such social functions around these parts, a golf tournament was to be the central event.

Now, Daddy had been known to wave a stick or two on that course, but had never really mastered the game. And to make this soon-to-be long story short, his 138 for 18 holes won him none other than your last place, by a long shot.

Hell, Daddy didn't really give a shit cause he thought the game was made to play for fun, or money if the strokes given were high enough to match the stakes.

But not this time. You see, his prize for coming in the farthest from the lead was an alleged autographed picture of old Adolf, himself, wearing a shit-eating grin and the words inscribed below it reading, "My County Wants You."

Mind you, this was all supposed to be in fun and I, myself, never having seen the picture, have no doubt that it was so. But what the good old boys hadn't counted on was the telegram Daddy received that afternoon after completing his not-so-valiant round.

See, both Daddy and Ted had been struck with the pang of patriotism when the war began, but one of them had to stay home and mind the store. Daddy, being the youngest, was left with that task. Brother Ted left to do the duty for both of them and almost made it.

That telegram, delivered to Daddy on that second Saturday in June 1944, told him how his only brother had lost his life on a beach in Normandy a few days before.

Mama told me how Daddy wasn't a vengeful man; however, that ill-timed reward was enough to set vengeance back a hundred years or more.

Old Leak swore he'd get even and after enough time had passed for mourning to clear, he did just that. He moved him and Mama from the Beverly Hills of Houston, up Highway 75, till he got to Conroe. From there he located and purchased one hundred acres of the most lush piney woods and proceeded to tear into that land until he had him the most hell-bent and dog-leg shittin' golf course that could bring even the lowest handicap golfer to his knees and screaming about giving his firstborn if he could just finish all 18 holes without the yellow stains meeting the brown in his Fruit-of-the Looms.

As the sign in front of the entrance reads:

THE CUT N SHOOT GOLF CLUB

(Bring your sticks and leave 'em)

***

As I left the make-shift press tent, courtesy of Jimmy's Rent All and Resale Shop over there on 105 near Thompson Lumber, I caught a casual glimpse of Thumper leaning over the cedar railing that surrounds the clubhouse's front porch and carrying on what looked to be a serious conversation with a set of tits you'd have to use a full wedge to reach the green from. Now, this ain't exactly uncommon for my best buddy of twenty-some odd years who's workin' on a bogey in the par 3 wife department.

It was a tough decision to make, but as his friend and long-time shoulder, I decided he needed a break from himself, so I ambled on over and asked the sweet thing to kindly forgive my intrusion but I needed a word with this gentleman, whom I'd heard was the owner of this wonderful piece of golf architecture and director of this outstanding tournament. I said I was sure he would find the time in his demanding schedule to work her in for some later, possibly unscheduled event. I could tell by the lack of sparkle in her eyes that my rude excuse had flown over her blonde head with no thought of landing.

"Shit! J.D! I think she kinda liked me." Thumper eased up from the railing and arched his back as he watched his favorite pair of that morning walk toward the bleachers being erected at the back of the Number 9 green.

"Yeah, and I'm sure she'll kinda like you a little bit better later on." It wasn't hard to imagine Thumper working on that one. I'd seen him with worse.

"Number 7," he said, before I was able to get back to the task at hand.

"Seven? Damn, Thump, that's a long way to walk."

"Shit, I gotta change the pin placement anyway. I might as well have company. Besides, seven's got the water and wind blowing through the pines."

The seventh hole just happens to be a 396-yard par 4 that pretty well borders the back part of the front nine. The fairway is lined by tall pines on the left and a lake on the right. What my good friend had in mind for the latter part of the evening was to have his way with his newfound pair on the right side of the seventh green, then transfer the cup from the right to the left. He was going to have to change the pin placement anyway, so our invited guests wouldn't be playing to the same pin in tomorrow's opening round. He would have eighteen changes to make before 8:00 A.M. I guess he does deserve the company.

"We got everybody in, do we?" Since I had been occupied the last hour or so with my buddies from the sports media, I hadn't been able to keep up with the arriving players, new and old. Since some of our so-called non-pros had never had the opportunity to play this course before and the returnees had not been allowed to either since this time last year, a practice round was a necessity if they hoped to survive.

I guess it's high time I explained this little tilt of ours before the players get down to the serious nut-cuttin'.

My Daddy always dreamed of putting on a golf tournament of some kind or another at Cut N Shoot, but he just never could quite figure out how to do it. Sure, when he first got the course built, he invited all those good old boys from Plantation Oaks to come by and play at the Grand Opening. He wanted to watch them shit in their knickers as their knees buckled, but only a few dozen showed and maybe only a half dozen of them finished.

After that, he opened the course up to the public and leased the operation to one of those golf course management companies until fourteen years ago. By that time, I was a freshman out in Lubbock. Daddy thought if I went to Texas Tech, I might locate his roots. I made the golf team and lettered three out of four years, while back in Conroe, my best buddy, Thumper Boone, was marrying his high school sweetheart of the last two months, Joy Beth Waters, and going to work as a greenskeeper at Daddy's golf course.

The rest is pretty much history. I tried to make it on the pro circuit, but quit after making the final cut in only one tournament in two years. Thumper got a divorce from Joy Beth and Daddy died.

He left the oil business and most of the money to Mama, with a stipulation that she sell it all off and live out the rest of her natural life in the luxury she damn sure deserved. He left The Cut N Shoot Golf Club to me and Thumper. I got 75% of the profit and old Thump got 25%, but he also got a hefty salary for running the place after the golf management's contract was not renewed. Now, Daddy wasn't trying to get back at me. It's just that Thumper had learned a lot in the previous six years on the course. He knew Mama would give me any of the money I wanted while she was alive and what was left out of what turned out to be a little over forty-three million dollars would go to me when she passed on.

And shit! What more did I need? I had my golf, Daddy's course and me and old Thumper were back together again.

The first thing we did after letting the management company go was selling all the gas riding carts and giving all the pull carts to the local Boys & Girls Club for their junior golf classes. WE also didn't allow either in the course. If you wanted to play Cut N Shoot, you had to play it on its terms. You walked and by God, you walked! We set the green fees at $25.00 a round. Weekdays, weekends, holidays; it didn't make shit. We did, however, supply caddies at $10.00 a round, plus tip, and the caddies got to keep it all. They did work, as we sure as hell didn't. And for the smart-ass golfer who thought he could carry his own clubs, we had caddies stationed at every tee box. However, to get one mid-stream like that costs you $15.00 to finish the round with them, plus tip. It was the price you paid for being a smart ass. The five-dollar difference went into a scholarship fund and each year, the high school senior caddies held their own two-day tournament and the winner received the proceeds, but it had to be used for college. You can take old Joe Don's word for it, THERE

ARE PLENTY OF SMART ASS GOLFERS IN THIS GREAT
STATE OF TEXAS!

Me and Thumper made a good living at Cut N
Shoot and I only had to hit Mama up for money
on one occasion. That was when the old barn we
used for a clubhouse burned down. Course, Mama
had every intention of paying for it anyway as
a Memorial to Daddy and Uncle Ted, which is
probably why it was a 50-year balloon note at
0% interest.

Me and Thumper knew we would someday live out
Daddy's dream of holding a golf tournament; we
just had to figure out the how-tos. And, ten
years ago, we did just that.

That first year, we limited the invitations
to fifty Texas players, plus myself as playing
host, based on the following rules:

> A player cannot be a member of any country
> club. A golf club, yes, but a country
> club, no. That was for Daddy.

> A player cannot be or have been a card-
> carrying professional golfer. Yours truly
> being the sole exception.

> A player must be a member of the National
> Golf Club, American Golf Club, United
> States Golf Club or some other recognized
> golfing organization with the facilities
> to maintain a computerized handicap.

> A player must have maintained within a
> plus or minus 2 of a scratch handicap over
> the past twelve months. However, the
> handicap must be at 0 within sixty days
> of the tournament.

The decision on the final participants are made solely by Thumper and myself.

That first tournament came and went with little notoriety other than the fact that it took the lovely little town of Cut N Shoot, population 569, almost two weeks to clear off the debris and clean up their daughters.

The second year was almost the same, although the invitees did get down to some serious partying and the cleanup took somewhat longer. It was shortly after that tournament that the Cut N Shoot Golf Club was hit with two suits naming us as a third party in divorces. Although the attorneys were the only ones who made money on those deals, it was then that me and Thumper came up with a further rule:

> A player's wife and family will not be allowed within 100 miles of Cut N Shoot during the tournament. Failure to comply will result in immediate expulsion and banishment from any and all future tournaments.

It was after The Cut N Shoot Classic III that we decided to open the invitations to the entire United States of America. It seems like we sort of pissed off our neighbors in Louisiana and Oklahoma. See, me and old Thump just didn't realize that word of our little get-together was spreading.

The format for Classic IV changed to include one player from each of the fifty states, plus the top ten finishers from the previous year. We were now hosting a field of sixty-one, due to my player-hosting, and the cleanup time took almost a month.

The results of Classic V took a different twist. Paternity suits, three total, entered the picture and cost us a pretty penny. However, thanks to insurance, we had the future covered.

There were no outstanding hitches to Classic VI. But VII was different. Me and Thumper invited a golfer from Arizona by the name of Randy Harpole. Damn good golfer too. However, when old Randy arrived, we found that her thighs reached all the way up to her ass. Randy turned out to be a Randi. She made it all the way to the finals on Sunday due to distractions only a serious golfer can understand. The golf god did, however, shine down upon us on the final day and saw fit to have her "friend" visit and her game went completely to shit, knocking her out of the top ten finishers, at number 13, and thus no automatic invitation the next year. We also decided that before sending out invitations in the future, we would call those we planned to invite to make sure they had the capability of singing baritone in the shower.

Thumper decided on another change for Classic VIII. Not that the tournament wasn't interesting enough, mind you, but just to liven up the festivities. On Thursday, the game would be match play rather than stroke, thus eliminating half the field after day one. Pairings would be drawn from the hat after the practice round on Wednesday. Friday, it would be back to stroke play with the twenty best scores going to the final two days play.

Man, it worked beautifully!

Classic IX saw no major changes other than our insurance rates skyrocketing. That year, the top ten finishers in order of their play and allowing them an automatic invitation to the coming free-for-all were:

Bubba Lee - Oklahoma

Lamar Malloy, Jr. - Texas

Tommy Smith - Florida

B.J. Littlejohn - Arizona

Ronnie Hurt - Pennsylvania

Tinker Brandt - Michigan

Beau Pritchett - Virginia

Kenji Yee - Hawaii

Walt Pearson - Wyoming

J.T. King - Massachusetts

I had finished 11th, thanks in part to a double bogey on the final hole. It was just as well, as being in the top 10 and also hosting would be a bit confusing next year. Since I had finished just out of the top ten, we then made the decision to allow eleven to enter the following year if I made it into the top ten.

Now that you all have a better than half-ass idea of what is about to transpire, we can continue on to The Cut N Shoot Classis X.

* * *

Now, according to Thumper, all the invitees to this year's event were presently somewhere out on the course, probably wishing they had stayed home and tickled their wife, girlfriend or both. Every once in a while, a faint echo of "sonofabitch" or "sgeeyut" could be heard bouncing off the pines and canyon walls, so we knew they had to be enjoying themselves. Either that or one of our infamous liquor cart ladies from over at Hazel's was catching a few of them by surprise and flashing a pair of better than amateur boobs during their backswing.

Thumper did mention that I, of course, was not out there and neither was Lamar Malloy, Jr. I knew that he knew that Lamar had come down from Dallas a day early and the two of us had gotten our once-a-year practice round in yesterday, before all the distractions showed up. This was just his way of showing me that he knew, that I knew, that he knew.

I decided that I would mosey back on over to see if the liquor tent, which acted earlier as the media tent, was being stocked properly and maybe even sample the wares like any good host would do under these same set of circumstances. However, this move was not to be, at least not yet. As I rounded the clubhouse, without undue haste, I nearly fell ass-over-teakettle on old Channel 3 Brucie sitting crossed-legged among the pine needles at the corner. He seemed to be lost in thought, which of course was unfamiliar territory for him, so I thought I had better than a double bogey chance of maybe passing on by without being noticed. But, uh uh.

"Mr. Buggs, you're just the one I wanted to see. Mind if I ask you a question?" That was another thing I semi-hated about the little prick. He never made eye contact when he talked. He was just sitting there like a Sioux Indian, wondering whether his squaw had been using his peace pipe to douche with. I had a good mind to tell him that if I was the one he wanted to see, he was in some bad shit on the trouble course. I wanted to tell him that with all the tour model tits and ass running around out there, surely he could find someone better than raggedly old me to shoot the shit with. But I remembered the TV contract and what my daddy used to tell me. "Son, if you can't say something good to somebody, then just shut the fuck up."

So, I bit my tongue and replied. "Yes, sir, Mr. Conlee. What can I do for you?"

He picked his body up and into a sort of upright position before he began his next sentence. "I, uh, had a chance to interview some of the players earlier and they were telling me I ought to mention how your wife helps organize this tournament and helps you every way she can. You know, I could make it sort of like one of those "Up Close and Personal" things like the network does. Would that be A-OK with you?"

It was all my middle-aged ass could do to keep from laughing beyond human control at his sincere, but obviously misguided, question. Thank goodness I was still carrying around my trusty putter that I had taken from my bag just before the press conference. I laid a left-handed grip on that sucker hard enough to sink an eighty-foot putt in the face of a blue norther. "Brucie, I don't want too much attention given to me in this here shindig."

I went on to tell him that he would probably get better sports-worthy stories by focusing on the other players themselves, as they were the ones who make up the tournament. Without them, there just wouldn't be one. I said there were a lot more of them than there was of me and that Billy Ray Breedlove would probably respect the hell out of him if he showed he had the ability to converse freely with the more athletic types in this here world.

Brucie said I was probably right and he thanked me for bringing that fact to his attention. I told him that it was the least I could do and that I again appreciated his taking up his valuable time to come up here and help us out the way he was doing. I told him there weren't many professionals in his line of work who would be so accommodating. And with that silver-tongued piece of undue praise, I gave him a little shoulder nudge to get him going in a direction opposite of mine, his gaze still never catching my baby blues.

Now, I knew damn well where that piece of information about my ex came from and it sure as shit wasn't from south of the Red River. Old Bubba Lee had done gone one up on me already.

It's true I was, or had been, married at one time, for a time. Holly Parker had frequented Classics III through V, although her knowledge of this Royal and Ancient game left a shit pot full to be desired. Our initial meeting left us both underwhelmed. I had just finished a less-than-spectacular third round in Classic III when this fiery redhead stepped from the piney shadows near the eighteenth green and asked me if I knew where a young lady might go to freshen up. Now, mind you, I was in no frame of mind to be cordial as I wasn't sure the 82 I had just carded would make the final cut. Therefore, my reply left us both a little stunned. I told her that I didn't think anyone had died and left me to be her tour guide and that if she needed a place to piss, there were plenty of pine trees on the back nine that the local deer didn't seem to mind using.

I hadn't stuck around for her reply, but later and after about a half dozen heavy scotches, I realized the error of my ways. It was about that time I felt a light tap on my shoulder.

"In a better mood yet, soldier?" She slid into the chair next to me with the ease of a pitching wedge from sixty yards out that had just landed on the green like a butterfly with sore feet.

"Not really," I replied. The scotch had done its trick on my silver tongue. It was obvious to her, although nothing was too damned obvious to me at the time, that if any decent conversation was to be had, she would have to do the leading.

She took control and apologized for entering my space earlier, as it was obvious I had my mind on other things more important than looking after the welfare of a stranger such as herself. I followed by actually apologizing for being so rude and even added that my comments were uncalled for; however, from what I remembered of our short visit, she didn't look one bit like she needed freshening up.

Things sort of clicked from there on, and after a less-than-whirlwind romance, two years of dating on and off, we tied the knot the day after I won Classic V. The only one I actually won.

It wasn't long afterward that it all started turning to shit. See, Holly Parker Buggs had come from one of your more well-to-do families over there in The Woodlands. Seems she had done some checking up on me before our actual not-really-chance meeting. She knew about my daddy's money, that was now my mama's money, that would someday be my money. When you got right down to it, she wasn't much more than your average run-of-the-mill, old road whore just looking for a bigger pot to piss in. The same kind my daddy used to warn me and Thumper about when we were young and in high school and had a hard time keeping old Charlie locked up behind the zipper. He would hear us bragging about our previous night's escapades or what we hoped to accomplish in the sex department later that evening and he'd come up behind us and kick us both in the ass, or at least try to. Usually, the second one to be kicked would have enough warning to be able to sidestep his aim. Then he'd say, "Look here, you two studs. I think both you should have had vasectomies when you were born, cause if you knock up one of those little sluts you been banging, I personally guarantee you will be fucked for life."

We hadn't been back in Conroe from our honeymoon over there in those Hawaiian Islands for no more than a month before she started hitting me up to get some of what she said was my rightful money from Mama. According to Thumper, I should have had enough sense to kick her ass out then and get the worthless marriage annulled. But, being eternally optimistic on my mama's side, I held on.

The clincher came at Classic VI. The bitch turned badass on me and tried her best to distract me from my once-a-year trial by fire. She knew that if yours truly failed to make the Top 10 finishers, I would be too embarrassed to play in my own tournament again. It was a touchy subject. She even went as far as feeding her redheaded lady-parts to one of the newcomer invitees, Max Wheeler from Delaware, in front of God and everybody, including me, late Saturday night out behind Turk's Longhorn Saloon. She called it too much liquor and I called it too much whore, then we both called our lawyers.

As usual, only the lawyers made any money on the divorce. She got the condo at April Sound and the Caddy Coupe, which didn't make shit to me as the car had been her wedding present anyway. In exchange, I got to keep my VW convertible, my golf clubs and my ownership in golf course; and probably best of all, she was forbidden to ever leave Highway 105 as she passed through Cut N Shoot, Texas. If she even signaled like she wanted to turn and go down Whipoorwill, old Zac Swick or either of his two young deputies were authorized by the court to throw her young, but well worn, ass behind bars. Oh yeah, she didn't even get to touch none of Mama's money either.

AT the time of her little escapade, I was six strokes behind the leader, Whitney Fontenot of Louisiana, but 13th in line. There was a six player log-jam in fourth place and two tied everywhere else, except first, fifth and of course sixth, where I sat.

All day Sunday, I just kept thinking of what my daddy used to tell me about this old game and how it pertained to life. He used to say, "Son, it don't matter how you play the game. What matters is if you win or lose. And that don't matter too damn much!"

I did manage to shoot a little over my head and finish still six strokes out of the lead. However, one-third of the players who had been ahead of me when the day began had thoroughly managed to shit in their own caps and sit back down in 'em. It had been Thumper's idea to switch from my basic white balls to optic orange ones. He said they would remind me of Holly's pussy and that, in itself, added twenty yards to each of my drives.

Anyway, I would be back as a player for Classic VII and Holly wouldn't.

Every year, my Okie buddy finds some way to remind me of my past experience on the marriage course. Every year, he gets a little downer and a little dirtier, but I always get even before the tournament ends.

* * *

I never did make it back to the liquor tent. Seems like whatever little nickel and dime problem that could arise, arose. Keith Fergus from Minnesota passed out from a heat stroke on the second rise of the Number 17 fairway. Calvin Carson of South Carolina tried to retrieve his Titleist from the water on Number 8, only to find his return path blocked by a family of irate cottonmouths. Blake Quantrell of California and Nate Kahil of New Hampshire almost went to fist city over whether Nate should be allowed a free drop when his drive on Number 14 came to rest inside the shell of a long-since-dead armadillo. But the most exciting event took place when Sandy Sanders of New Mexico got in such a hurry to see where his shot ended up on Number 9 that he lost his footing and went over the edge of the tee box. It was a life-or-death struggle there for a while, but with the help of the KHSN camera crew, who were setting up their equipment for Saturday using a rental crane, they were able to pluck Sandy down from his perch high above the green. He ended up with a triple bogey, which wasn't bad considering what might have been. Golfer that old Sandy was, he did agree to allow those behind him to play through, so as not to slow up play.

This is the time of the tournament I always enjoy. WE got your Texas-style barbecue being manufactured by Cut N Shoot's own Stumpy Brown, owner of Stumpy's, also over there on Highway 105. Everything in Cut N Shoot is either on or off 105, except our little hundred acres and Patsy's Roller Rink and Bingo Hall over there on Loop 336. And, of course, the houses of those five hundred and some odd folks who call Cut N Shoot home.

While Stumpy was working his magic, the alcoholic attitude adjustments were flowing. The forest was ringing with the bitchin' from those whose knees buckled as the course brought them down earlier, as well as the braggin' of those who fared well enough on the greenies, skinnies, bingo-bango-bongos or what-have-you to cover whatever expenses they may have had in arriving at our little out-of-the-way location.

The gambling was just getting started. You see, the Cut N Shoot Classic is an amateur event, which means there ain't no prize money being offered. However, there ain't a golfer in this here world that will play the game without stakes of some sort being involved, and this tournament of ours is definitely no exception. A man has been known to finish in 9th or 10th place and cart home the long green in five figures. In Classic VIII, one of the second ten finishers pocketed near twenty-five grand from his fellow players, which beat those in the top three by a good ten grand. His name will obviously not be spoken for reasons known only to hisownself and the IR of S.

But right now it was party time. Hazel's girls were making their rounds, trying to separate the winners from the losers and the winners from some of, if not all, their day's winnings. There weren't none of them gonna be given a chance to take the cash home to Mama. Not if Hazel's Honeys could help it.

At this very moment, though, all the invitees were amongst the perpendicular. It was time for the drawing for tomorrow's pairings.

Thumper was already on the make-shift stage under the tent with a firm grip on his old Conroe High football helmet, crammed full of each and every driver's license of each and every player. They sure as hell wouldn't need them since we took away their car keys at the registration desk that morning. The town fathers liked to keep the roads as safe as possible, which was no problem since Hazel's girls also doubled as chauffeurs along with their other duties. Me and Thumper had to live in this town the other fifty-one weeks out of each and every year, and although we couldn't keep their daughters safe, we could keep the roads secure. Hazel and her crew did a fair to middlin' job keeping the daughters out of female trouble.

"Buford! Get your ass up here, boy!" Thumper had heard through the grapevine of Bubba's little conversation with Brucie concerning Holly's alleged management of our tournament and he was about to bring me and Bubba to even on our match-play of words. See, old Bubba don't like to advertise his true Christian name laid upon him by his mama, but he was about to get a little of what we will call free publicity, courtesy of my longtime buddy and friend.

As Bubba climbed up next to Thumper with all-knowing fire in his eyes, old Thump continued. "Folks, this here is Buford Elmo Lee from none other than Texas north or Oklahoma, as the residents of his homeland are used to calling it. Buford here just happens to be the defending champion of this here shindig. And with that honor comes the prize of being able to draw for tomorrow's pairings for match play. Now, without further ado, I give you Buford Elmo Lee."

The applause was so un-deafening you could have heard a Maxfli bite back on Number 7 green.

"Eat a dick, Thumper," Bubba whispered as he jammed his hand into the helmet still in the grasp of the one wearing the big shit-eating grin.

"Blake Quantrell, California and Nelson Ulrich, Indiana." As Bubba read out the names, Hazel and Melanie, her number one employee, began placing the names and states onto the leader board outside the tent. They got to my name about midway through the drawing, pairing me with a newcomer, Pepper Cain from Rhode Island. Bubba grinned like a Cheshire cat when he read his victim's name; another newcomer, Red McMichaels from Nebraska. A grudge match for bragging rights, if there ever was one.

It wasn't hard for me to locate Pepper, as he was the first one to belly up to the temporary bar the minute he heard I was to be his foe. I decided that it was time to start the ritual of psyching out my opponent, so I gave him time to bottom out his first rum and coke before I put my arm across his shoulder and asked if it took him as long to walk his home state, border to border, as it did this fine course of ours. He didn't answer as he reached for his second Bacardi, downed it and requested a third. If he kept that up all right, I would be able to play the round with nothing but my trusty putter.

Probably the most interesting pairings brought J.T. and Kelly Dale together again. The two weren't exactly strangers, not because they had played together in the practice round, but because they had gone head to head several times up there in New England. J.T., of course, was one of the top ten finishers last year, so he had a slight advantage on the course layout. However, Kelly was younger and stronger, which is a definite plus here at Cut N Shoot. Kelly was probably the best looking of the sixty competitors, which is probably why he was surrounded most of the time by many of Hazel's finest, not to mention a few of the local daughters. Old J.T. noticed that right off and as all good golfers know, sex, especially a night crammed full of it, does tend to drain a player's sap, not to mention his energy. J.T.

felt even more at ease when he saw Melanie brush the other girls aside and latch onto Kelly after she had placed the last pairing on the board. Beau Pritchett, Virginia and Sandy Sanders, New Mexico.

At least Sandy would have a little more time to recuperate from his near-death experience at Number 9. Being drawn last meant he didn't have to tee off until 12:50 pm tomorrow. He would need the rest as Beau finished seventh last year as a rookie at Cut N Shoot. He could hit a mean, straight drive that very seldom found trouble.

"That's a first," Thumper told me as he leaned on the bar next to me, empty helmet in hand.

"What's that?" I questioned, taking a first sip of my newfound scotch.

"None of last year's boys got paired up with each other."

"You figure that'll make for easy pickings?" Thumper was well acquainted with the invitees, although he had seen only a few of them actually play. Old Thump studied the printouts on all of them as well as their home courses before he made his choices each year, so he had a better than half-ass idea of what they could do here at Cut N Shoot.

"For you, maybe, but Tinker is gonna have his hands full with Taylor from Florida." Spook Taylor had won just about every major event his state had to offer. He had shot below par at both Seminole and the Tournament Players. The only reason he had never turned pro was the traveling. He was deathly afraid of flying and there was no way in hell he could drive to enough tournaments and still meet the minimum allowed by the PGA. He didn't need the money anyway since his daddy owned more Ford dealerships in Florida than all the others put together. He just played golf at his leisure and lived off his old man. By the way, Spook was his real given name. You see, he had died the very second he popped out from his mama from some type of congenital heart failure. It had taken the doctors a little under five minutes to bring him back, a birdie on anyone's par 5. His daddy, being a man of an extreme sense of humor, decided the name fit the occasion, although his mama thought Casper would have been much more appropriate and appealing.

"What about this Dale kid? Will King be able to handle him?" I noticed, as the words were rolling out, that the one for whom I was speaking was nowhere to be seen. Nor was Melanie, for that matter.

"Toss up," Thumper responded. "Depends on how much J.T. has slipped into Melanie's pocket."

I guess it is like what's always been said about all being fair in love and war. If you love winning at this silly game of golf enough to go to war over it, you're willing to pay the price.

Thumper leaned back from the bar and started gazing out over the masses under the tent. "Who you looking for, old buddy?" I asked.

"My helper. You know, Miss Prize Tits 1987. I got me some pin placements to change." No sooner had he finished his sentence than he was off. About half an hour later, I spotted him in one of our only golf carts heading for the front nine with the lovely pair sitting next to him, and his cup sucker leaning in the back golf bag section.

J.T. King was still under the tent, wearing a shit-eatin' grin and I was about to make the rounds in search of something strange. After all, I had me a golf match tomorrow to prepare for.

T H U R S D A Y

MATCH-PLAY, ME AND MELANIE

Breakfast is served in the liquor tent beginning at six-thirty and ending, well, whenever Miss Lucy wants it to end. The difference between our little get-together and those high-falootin' tournaments the big boys put on for money and fame is that we do all the providin'. The only thing our guests need to worry about having to pay for are your common, every day, run-of-the-mill, professional playthings. Now that ain't to say that we don't have enough of the strange, free stuff hanging around the course. It's just that the golfer needs to know how to read the break.

Anyway, and like I was saying, being that there ain't no prize money awarded and these guys play the game for kisses and fucks, we try to make it so all they got to think about in the game of golf, cause when you get right down to it, that's sort of why they are here.

So, we got Miss Lucy of Lucy's Highway Grill handling the breakfast menu, which usually carries your normal every day morning staples of biscuits, gravy, grits, scrambled eggs, bacon, sausage, fresh fruit and fruit juice, hash browns and enough coffee to wake the dead or dying. And for the light eater, she carries an assortment of pastries and them little cereal boxes that spill all over your crotch when you try to open 'em up.

Dinner is supplied by the Kuntry Kichun. Yep, over there on 105, same as Miss Lucy's. This meal is usually made up of assorted sandwiches, fresh fruit and Snickers, for energy, mind you. These are available at the liquor tent, in case you have finished your round; otherwise, an ample supply is delivered to each tee box for the patrons of the course to eat at their leisure.

And supper is in the hands of good old Stumpy, whom I have spoken of before.

Now we usually manage to fuck up a couple of the players from the other side of the Mason-Dixon line, whose mamas taught 'em to call dinner lunch and supper dinner. When they ask for lunch, we just tell 'em it was served at breakfast.

No matter which meal or in-between meal is being served, the bar is still open. We got that sucker manned from six in the morning till midnight. During those other six hours, the players are free to serve themselves.

Just the other side of Whipoorwill, and at the opposite end of Crystal Creek as our golf club, is Smokey's Hideaway, the home of seventy-five of the most rustically, scenic cabins in all of the Texas piney woods. Each cabin is hidden in its own seclusion, giving the golfer complete freedom of solitude, which is a necessity during tournament time. After all, he may not want any of the others to know which one of Hazel's lovelies was taking his money. You see, golfers by nature are a superstitious lot.

I assume you would like to know who is footing the bill for all this, as me and old

Thumper surely can't be making enough to carry all that till tax time. Well, Mama decided that since it was Daddy who had the original dream for a tournament and since I was a good enough son to play out his dream, the least she could do was bankroll the operation.

So, like I promised, if the golfer didn't favor none of our local ladies, he had no need for money at this here tournament.

Now, of course, bettin' don't count. That ain't considered money to be spent. No golfer alive who has ever bet a quarter and lost would consider that as spent money. It's an investment in the future. Before you can win money, you gotta bet money. If that don't make sense to you, then you got no business even playing this silly game or any other game for that matter. The thrill of victory comes and goes, but with money dances the dog.

I left my piece of strange in cabin twelve and headed for the course about the time the sun was coming up over Cleveland. That would be Cleveland, Texas. It sits right where 105 crosses 59, just east of here. Thumper was already out surveying the course when I arrived. Either that or he was just coming in from Number 7. Since he was alone, I figured it was probably the former. Lucy was hard at it, but she cracked her usual smile behind her Winston and then kept on keeping on. There was a slight fog hanging on the course, which was usual for this time of June, and it painted the sort of picture that makes it damn well worth getting up at this hour. It sort of makes you glad to be alive and standing on a golf course.

As I sat down for a cup of Lucy's coffee, I heard a familiar voice enter the tent behind me. "Yo, Joe Don. I see you had no trouble in rounding up a cot partner last night."

"Howdy, Lamar. Now that I think about it, I don't remember seeing you at the pairings last night. You don't give a rat's ass who you play today?" I really hadn't seen Lamar since our practice round on Tuesday, when, by the way, I beat him by two strokes. We did, however, tie for match-play.

"Aw shit, son. I had me some urgent business to attend to over in Houston yesterday, but I got back in just enough time to see you leaving with that redhead. Looks to me like you got yourself a death wish. I was sure you had sworn off redheads for life." Lamar's business was either his girlfriend over in Katy or some honest-to-goodness real estate deal he usually has going. You just never know with Lamar.

"She was only red on top. She was brunette where it counts. You better get on over there and take a look at the leader board because I can't seem to remember who you go against or when." After I caught my own pairing, I hadn't paid much attention to the others. I figured they were all big boys and could take care of themselves.

"Hunter Agajanian from Alaska at nine-fifty sharp. Melanie filled me in last night during evening workouts." Lamar filled his cup and grabbed a plate of biscuits and gravy with bacon on the side, both of which he proceeded to drown in pepper.

"Melanie? Hazel's Melanie?" I don't know whether I asked the question for my own benefit or J.T.'s.

"That's the only one I know. She met me at Cissie's over in Conroe for supper and left when I did a while ago. I know you don't like to have to pay for your stuff, son, but you ought to give her a try sometime. Shit, she ain't half bad for a pro. Besides, you ain't got to worry about them AIDS with her. You know, Hazel keeps all them girls clean."

"Fuck AIDS!" I meant that too. I'd rather bite the big one from that disease than cancer. Daddy died of cancer and he hurt like shit for too long a time. "If I found out I had cancer, I'd go get me a heavy AIDS injection so I could die from that first," I told him.

"Whatever. I don't have no hankering to die of anything right now. I got too much golf left in me to play. If I ever get to the point where I can't play this here game, then you can let 'em inject me with horseshit if you want to, cause I'd be better off dead." What old Lamar said made quite a lot of sense, even at this early hour of the day. When you really get to thinking about it, most avid golfers would rather be dead than medically banned from the links.

"Did Melanie say anything about a golfer name Kelly Dale?" I had to ask, cause I had a feeling that young Pepper Cain wasn't going to provide much of a challenge for me today, so I needed to find something else to focus my unused attention on.

"Yeah, as a matter of fact, she did. As soon as she sat down at Cissie's, she said something about J.T. King was about to be the recipient of some serious golf fucking. She said something about having to return a couple of hundred green ones to J.T., but I wasn't paying too much attention. You understand I did have other things on my mind at the time. Why?"

"Nothing other than old J.T.'s probably done psyched himself right out of this tournament before it even starts." If Melanie got to J.T. before tee time, then he might as well just call in the dogs and piss on the fire. If she didn't, then he might have a fighting chance. But, since it wasn't my fight, I had no intention of getting involved any further than I already was.

It was nearing seven and the tent was filling up. I managed to throw down some dry scrambled eggs and a couple bowls of grits, smothered in butter, between idle chit-chat with some of the newcomers. Mostly, they would ask me for some pointers and what to look for and look out for on the course. I told them to look for Hazel's girls and look out for timber rattlers. I told 'em I was a player in this here tournament and I wasn't about to give away no trade secrets to someone I might be facing the next day.

Kelly Dale showed up five minutes before his tee time, went straight to the bar and threw down a quick beer and then headed for Number 1. I followed along behind, mainly because I didn't have anything better to do at the moment. Melanie was standing next to a tanish pale J.T. King, so my question was answered. Kelly offered J.T. the honors as if leading him to slaughter, and J.T. accepted with dignity.

Now, for those of you who have not yet had the opportunity to play Cut N Shoot, Number 1 is the easiest hole on the course. Even a bogey golfer has a better than good chance for a par and a good golfer, a birdie. All you gotta do is drive the ball straight. It is a 305 yard par four, downhill to a level green. The fairway is lined with tall pines and a small creek meanders out of play in front of the tee box. Sand traps horseshoe around the back of the green, but the fringe is cut short enough to allow a good driver to be able to putt from off the green and a better-than-good driver to drive the green. The only problem there is the level green does not aid in stopping too huge a hit. My daddy started the course this way to give the golfers a false sense of security.

J.T. took a heroic stab at his ball and knocked it straight into the creek that isn't supposed to come into play. He gained back a little confidence when he drove his second shot, which counted as his third, onto the green. Kelly, however, drove to the front of the green and two-putted for a birdie, making him one up with seventeen left to play, and J.T. hadn't even got to putt yet.

I walked on over to the clubhouse to see if Thumper needed me for anything before I got ready to play. He said he didn't and that he wasn't trying to show favoritism, but that I should keep my approach shot on Number 7 away from the right side of the green. I told him I had planned on doing that anyway. I told him I had known him for too many years to even consider him being a failure at something so trivial as getting laid. He wished me luck and I left to prepare for the event.

I took a look in the tent on my way back by, but there was still no sign of Pepper. I thought about calling Smokey's to see if they would check on him in case he had died or something, but I put that thought out of my head and went on with my own preparation.

Pepper Cain showed up just before ten, which gave him just a hair more than half an hour to get some of Lucy's best into his stomach before he had to face me. I decided to leave him to himself for his last half hour.

I called it close to right. After twelve holes, I was seven up with six left, so it was all over but the crying. I asked Pepper if he wanted to play on in and he said yes. After that, he played like a champ. With no more pressure involved, the kid beat me five out of the last six holes. So, the posted score showed me to be the winner, two up. I told him that if he went back out tomorrow, head-to-head, he would probably beat me. But as it stood, I won and he lost and it all boiled down to killer instinct. I had it and he didn't; at least not yet.

I decided to drop by the leader board and maybe grab a cool scotch before getting out of my spikes. Melanie was posting my two-up but that wasn't what caught my eye, nor was it Melanie's firm buttocks as they inched out of her white short-shorts, as she leaned across the board to show that Ronnie Hurt of Pennsylvania had just inched out Kyle Smoot of Utah by one up. Placed to the left of Kelly Dale's name was a 10*. I asked Melanie the meaning of the asterisk.

"Kelly put J.T. down in ten. I mean ten straight holes. J.T. wouldn't even have been able to muster up a tie. Penny was walking the round with them and she said J.T. walked to Number 11 tee box mumbling something about having his dodo packed with a flag-stick, reached for his bag like he was going to grab his club to tee off, then grabbed the entire bag, walked to the small pond off to the left of the box and threw his clubs into the water. He then proceeded to drop his pants and moon in all four directions before hovering over the pond and mooning his clubs. Damn, I wish I could've seen that!" She went on to tell me that Kelly had J.T.'s caddie get his clubs out of the water and carry them back to the clubhouse. Meanwhile, Kelly finished his round by himself with Penny and his caddie in tow, grabbed another quick beer in the liquor tent, then walked on over across Whirlpool to Smokey's.

"You were with him a while. What do you think makes him tick?" I had this funny feeling like I had better learn all I could about this kid from Connecticut. At least as far as his game of golf was concerned.

"Well, I can damn sure tell you he ain't interested in a sure thing. At least he wasn't yesterday." Rachel handed Melanie another scorecard, allowing her to again offer me a view of her anatomy as she wrote that Jubal Washington of Georgia, our first black golfer, had beaten Justin Lord of Texas, four up. That meant Jubal must be one hell of a golfer, as Justin looked to me and Thumper to be the best Texas had to offer this year.

I walked on over to the clubhouse, cleaned up my Footjoys and put them in my locker. Thumper wasn't around, so I would have to wait until later to thoroughly question him about young Mr. Dale. I went on back over to Cabin 12 and saw my partner from the previous evening had left, so I showered and jumped in between the sheets to grab a couple of winks before returning to the evening action.

* * *

Other than old J.T.'s demise at the hands of Kelly, there were no real massacres. Seven of last year's finishers survived the first round of match-play. Other than J.T., only Tinker Brandt and Walt Pearson were left out in the cold. Thumper had been right about Spook Taylor, and according to Tinker, the boy don't belong on the amateur circuit. L.B. "Pudge" McMoon of Arkansas had managed to take Walt out on the last hole. They had tied the previous seventeen. We also had two sudden deaths in the round. One being my good buddy, Lamar, who will never take an Alaskan golfer for granted again. He finally won on Number 3, when he got on the par 3 green with his drive and Hunter Agajanian hit his over the green and into the water. Hunter conceded the hole at that point, which is allowable in match play. The other involved two newcomers, Ricky Pinchon from South Dakota and D.D. Rappaport from Maine. That one only lasted one hole with D.D. coming out on top, thanks in part to a 20 foot putt that circled the rim before dropping in the back door for a birdie.

Old Bubba had his hands full with his Nebraska counterpart, but still managed to finish two up. "Shit, Joe Don, I wasn't never

37

worried. It was in the bag the whole time. I was just funnin' with him, that's all."

"Uh, huh. And how many Jacks is that you've put away so far, old stud?" As far as I could tell, Bubba was pretty shaken at having such a close call on the course. He had been hitting the Jack Daniels straight fairly heavily since I arrived and I don't know how long he had been at it before then.

"Six or twelve, but who's counting? Say, when's Thumper gonna be here so we can get the pairings drawn for tomorrow?" At that precise moment, old Thumper was back in the clubhouse separating the winning drivers' licenses from the losing drivers' licenses. By all counts, it should be thirty-thirty. Tomorrow's round would begin the three-day stroke-play. The golfers would no longer be playing head-to-head, but rather playing against the scorecard. The top twenty scores would advance to both weekend rounds. The remaining ten could go home or stay, if they liked. They just couldn't play golf, that is. The pairings had no real bearing on the outcome, except maybe for betting purposes. If you liked to play for big money, you always hoped to be paired with someone of similar taste. Some golfers felt that they played a better game when teamed with a better golfer, so they hoped to draw someone like B.J. Littlejohn or Lamar, or Bubba or even me. Others liked to play against someone they could beat the shit out of. It seemed for those types that the worse they were beating someone, the better they got. Me, hell, I just play against the course.

As Thumper waltzed into the tent with Conroe High under his right arm, I looked around to

see if I could catch a glimpse of Kelly Dale.
All I had to do was look for a swarm of women
and there he was. His eyes caught mine in a
steady glare and then he winked just like the
fucker knew something that I didn't. I had to
make sure I got hold of Thumper as soon as the
pairings were drawn. I thought surely the kid
wasn't trying to work a psyche on me. Or maybe
he was.

Since Bubba had pretty well behaved himself
over the last twenty-four hours, Thump decided
to leave him to his Jacks and get someone else
to draw the pairings. He said that since last
year's winner had drawn yesterday, then it was
only fitting that the one who had won the match-
play by the biggest margin should draw for
tomorrows. With that, he called young Dale up
on the platform with him, while looking me
square in the eye.

Kelly didn't say a word. Not one damn word.
When he drew the first license, he handed it
to Thumper to read. The boy wasn't going to
give nothing away. The first pairings were
Mikey Lo Bianco of New Jersey and Butch Bonner
of Alabama. They would start the round at ten
in the morning and the rest of us would follow
at fifteen-minute intervals. I got paired with
another newcomer in Adrian Hodges of Missouri,
again midway through the draw. Bubba still
didn't get matched too far away from home. He
got to play against another Okie, Kenny Winner.
The two of them had played in a couple of
tournaments together, but never head-to-head,
so to speak. According to Bubba, Kenny had only
scored lower than him on one occasion. I asked
him if that meant he was not going to take
tomorrow's match too seriously and he advised

me that he would be ready. At least I think that's what he said. The Jack Daniels seemed to be filling his mouth with marbles.

Lamar was paired with a yankee from New York, Sam Werlinger. I knew Lamar would be ready, cause now it was down to him against the world, or at least 29 of its residents.

Kelly Dale drew himself Dean Shillings from Wisconsin and smiled when he did it. For Dean's sake, I hoped he was the kind who played good golf when he was playing with a good golfer. Or maybe I didn't. After all, ten people on that leaderboard would not be allowed to play after tomorrow. One of them might as well be him, rather than me.

Stumpy had fried up a mess of catfish for the evening meal, along with some deep-fried French fries to grease the way for what we were about to throw down stomach-way later tonight at Turk's Longhorn Saloon. Even after Holly's floor show a couple of years back at that establishment, I still managed to show my face on occasion. It had been on the Thursday nights in the previous years that the paternity suits had spawned. It is the night after the first cut, so those who had to pack their clubs up have nothing to lose. It's on Thursday nights that the town fathers lock their daughters in their attics where there ain't no windows for them to crawl out of. Some of them do manage to escape, however, and usually live to regret it.

Hazel's car caravan left for Turk's about eight. I told them I would meet them there and Melanie stayed around to make sure I did just that. Her reason was that I was a player in this here tournament, so I also had to play by the rules, which meant I was not allowed to drive. I learned a long time ago that it was easier to try and correct a slice than to try and correct a woman.

My reason for staying behind was to corner Thumper and pick his brain about the now ever mindful Kelly Dale. I found Thump over in the tool shed, laying an edge to his cup-sucker. "I see you managed to make it through the hard part alive," he told me, not looking up from his task at hand.

"Yeah, but that kid will make it. We'll be seeing his name on the TV leaderboards in a couple of years."

"I know for a fact that you ain't here to give me no help with tomorrow's pin placements, but I got me a pretty good idea about what the topic of our conversation is gonna be, so I will tell you right now that the answer is just beat the course."

"You could have at least waited till I asked the question."

"Didn't need to. I saw you lookin' at that Dale kid. If I were you, and of course I'm not and you probably ain't gonna listen to me anyway, but since you're here, I'm gonna tell you. Just play your own fuckin' game and don't worry about them others, especially him. You got the advantage here cause you've probably played this course of your daddy's more than several hundred times more than any of them. You know how Psyche works cause you've worked it and if you let some young shit come in here and turn the tables on you, then by God, you deserve to get your ass whipped. And don't forget, old buddy, once you don't make the cut, then you're probably out for good. You sure as hell won't get my vote as a newcomer."

Although I wasn't looking for a lecture from Thumper, I sure got one. And he was right. Still, I wanted more for my money. "Just give me some facts to work on and let me handle my game."

"OK. Fact number one is that he can and will whip your ass if you give him half a chance. He was All American at Wake Forest his last two years and single-handedly kicked the living shit out of U of H last year. He stands 5'9" and tips the scales at a lean and mean 165 pounds, dripping wet. He has blonde hair, green eyes and would be a dream fuck for any of the bitches we got runnin' around here. I don't know the length of his dick, but if you really want to know, I'll put Miss Prize Tits on it and see what she can find out. What other facts you want, son?" Thumper still hadn't looked up from his work and that old cup-shucker would surely be able to cut through most anything by now.

"Why hasn't he turned pro? And why are you pissed off at me?"

"I ain't pissed off at you. I've just never seen you get so screwed up about one of our golfers. And word is that he wanted to play in this tournament before he went for the big money."

"Now that just don't make a hell of a lot of sense and that means you damn sure know something else you're not sharing with me."

Thumper laid his tools down and walked over to the fridge next to the back door and pulled out two Lone Star longnecks. As usual, he placed the edge of the caps on the metal workbench and slammed his hand down on them, popping both tops at once. He offered one to me, a sign that I had better sit down and listen up. "This kid grew up not far from here, but just before high school, his family moved up to Connecticut, where he honed his golfing skills on some of your better courses. I wasn't altogether truthful about him wanting to play in this tournament. It was really his daddy who wanted him to."

"OK, so big deal. We got us a local boy whose daddy wants him to come back home and make good. Where's he from, Conroe? Huntsville? Montgomery? Where?"

"Houston."

"I still don't see the problem, and if you are going to screw up my taste buds by making me sit here and drink this beer when I could be playing at Turk's, then I'm leaving right now."

"Houston, as in Plantation Oaks."

All of a sudden, the world became crystal clear. Daddy's revenge had come full circle. "Wouldn't that have made his daddy a little young to have been involved with that group?"

"Yeah, except he had him one of those May-December second marriages and we're sittin' here talking about the by-product."

"So, then it **is** me against him. No matter how you look at it. He's here to beat me."

"Well, asshole, as usual, you ain't heard one damn word I said. It's you against the course. You beat the course, you beat him. There ain't no difference between this or any other tournament. You beat the course; you don't beat the players."

Old Thumper was mostly right; however, if all you had to do was beat the course, then the old golf god wouldn't have invented psyche. It was all going to boil down to whether a 38 year old, almost has-been could deliver the fatal blow to a pup half his age. But that's the way golf is supposed to be. It's a sport where age is not necessarily a factor. There is no physical contact with the players, only with a little round ball with several dozen dimples.

"Does Mama know?"

"Nope. And she won't if you win."

"Thanks a lot."

"Just play your game, Joe Don. Just play your game."

My beer had become too warm to drink, but I didn't like beer anyway. I remembered that Melanie was outside waiting for me, so I excused myself. When I got to the door, I decided I better let old Thump know that I understood what needed to be done. "Don't worry, Thump. I may not win this tournament of ours, but I'll damn sure beat him."

"That ain't good enough, slick. You're gonna have to win this thing to beat him." He picked up his cup-shucker and headed for the back door, knowing he was right.

★★★

Turk's Longhorn Saloon was beyond a doubt the night spot of Cut N Shoot. Why folks came from as far as New Caney just to listen and dance to the R&R-C&W sounds of Jake Shiloh and his Hideaway Dirt Band. Hell, tonight there was a hundred plus crowding the dance floor. Some came for the décor and others for the music, but mostly it's the dollar well drinks and fifty-cent beer.

Melanie led me across the dance floor packed with tan, young, stud-looking dudes, all decked out in Jaymar beltless slacks and colorful Sahara shirts with little illegible emblems above the pockets or on the left sleeves. It wasn't hard to distinguish the pros from the strange either. Hazel had purchased three dozen of Cut N Shoot Golf Club's ladies' golf shirts for her girls. All maroon solids with the crossed Colt Pistol and Bowie knife emblem sewn right above the left breast. Hazel said something about not being able to tell the players without a program. There were probably half as many strange wandering about, which meant that some of the invitees would probably go home empty handed. But the night was still young, although some of us weren't, we just acted like it.

To say the least, the dance hall was ours, and we intended on keeping it. I noted that my partner from the previous evening had made the trek and was holding Spook Taylor in abeyance. I could rightfully say that she wouldn't hurt Spook's game none. I was also glad that I hadn't seen Miss Prize Tits here on the scene. That was a good sign that Thumper still had him a pin placement helper tonight.

A quick headcount told me we had a few stragglers, but their names escaped me, save one. I somehow knew Kelly Dale would not be joining this happy throng.

Turk's was your usual Texas dance hall. Hardwood floors, high knotty-pine beamed ceiling, deer trophies mounted about the pine walls and loud, loud music. It was easy to tell who among us were not from the southwest, as they seemed to be in awe of the place. A couple more cheap drinks and they would feel like they were born here. I also noticed that Turk's had a new piece of furniture leaning against one of the two bars. One of our players, probably one of today's lucky winners, had confiscated the leaderboard. I hoped old Tommy "Turk" Luchesse understood that possession ain't necessarily nine-tenths of the law in these parts, cause it took me and Thumper a good day to get that sucker built a few years back.

It didn't take Jake and his boys too long to get this show on the road. They started off with their rendition of The Rose just to get everyone relaxed and in touch with their true emotions, plus other things. I did Melanie a favor and slid across the floor with her for the first number and actually came in touch with a nice, if not unfamiliar, emotion. When they broke into the Cotton Eyed Joe, I decided it was time for me to sit down. That dance tune could easily result in a few broken legs if left to amateurs to perform. With Hazel's girls, aided by a few strange, acting as dance instructors, our happy horde tripped the light fantastic until the song ended and then had old Jake play it again for good measure.

As the night wore on, some of the locals joined us, probably just to catch our act. Lamar figured they were there to make sure none of their daughters had made it to freedom.

The highlight of the evening came when Arizona's best, B.J. Littlejohn, challenged Nevada's proud son, Chris Carmichael, to an old fashioned twist-off. Mind you, this came in the wake of the Hideaway Dirt Band's infamous set of fifties and sixties music. Now, neither one of these young bucks had yet to hit the quarter-century mark in their ages, so to say the least, they have this famous dance a bad name for those of us who were weaned on the step. Their chosen partners, Kathi and Cathi, Hazel's moon dust twins, were able to keep the eye action focused in their direction, thus the saving grace for the boys. Others in the group joined in as Jake stretched the song to the limit, and everyone agreed that the winner, by better than a default, was none other than Jubal Washington, who had not even been in on the original challenge. Not that anyone even remembered as far back as the beginning of the set.

Since Holly was an injunctioned no-show, the evening came to a close, at least at Turk's, with no lasting event that would leave a bad taste in anyone's mouth, either physically or literally.

With the alcohol consumption level at a record-breaking high, I had my doubts that much pre-marital or extra-marital sex would be on the menu in Smokey's cabins tonight. Most likely there would be a little kissy-face and huggy-body after the money changed hands, but that would be quickly followed by the snoring

of the well-intentioned males of the species.
It didn't really matter cause they would never
be the wiser, and like most golfers, they would
be too vain to ask questions in the morning.
Most of them wouldn't even be able to remember
who drove them home and tucked them in, or set
their travel alarm clocks for seven a.m. Either
way, the girls had earned their money.

I decided to take Lamar's suggestion, so when
Melanie drove us up in front of Cabin 12, I
invited her on in. After deciding the
atmosphere was not to our liking, we took a
blanket out of the cedar-lined closet and laid
it out on the ground below the wind-swept
pines. We talked for a while, mostly about life
in general. Neither of us brought up the
subject of the other's chosen profession, which
was just as well. We did finally make love, not
mad passionate love as you would have expected,
but passionate still.

A light rain shower woke us up about three
a.m., so we moved back on inside where we made
love again to the sound of rain on the cedar
shake roof. I fell asleep thinking of how the
early morning rain would make my approach shot
to the greens bite and hold.

When my alarm woke me at seven, she was gone.

STROKE-PLAY, SCOTCH AND THE CRYSTAL PISTOL

The rain had only been a late spring shower. Thumper had a small crew out on the course, whipping the greens when I arrived. I was glad to see that Turk had permitted the return of the kidnapped leader board, although it had not yet been returned to its perch next to the tent. I had no doubt Thumper would take care of that little chore before the first scores of the day were to be posted.

The sun had already cleared the top of the pines and the aroma of Lucy's breakfast hung about the tent like yesterday's fog. A fair trade in my book. I sat down with my usual coffee, cream, but no sugar. Lamar and a handful of others had beat me in, so I sat down next to him and, from the sweat that was already gleaming about his forehead, I knew he had risen early and walked the course in search of the newly laid pin placements.

"I think our old buddy, Thumper, is trying to put the Johnson bar to us today, hoss." He slid his small notepad my way for review. With the exception of Number 9, Thumper had tucked each and every flagstick behind a front bunker or up close to the water on the left front of all the greens.

"It's definitely gonna separate the men from the boys," I said.

"No shit! And some of the boys from their Pinnacles. Look what he did on Number 6." I didn't have to look. Thumper did this every year. He made sure that the boys would quickly forget the previous day's round by placing the cups so close to the front hazards that no one would dare shoot for the pin itself. It put one-putting on the endangered species list, if not making it totally extinct.

"It's just old Thump's way of showing us that we don't play the course, it plays us."

"I got something Thumper can play with."

"What's the matter, Lamar? You have to sleep with just your teddy bear last night?"

"Yeah, but by choice. I have an idea you didn't though. Was I right?"

"Let's just say the saying about learning from your elders still holds true."

"Well, just you don't forget that your mama taught you to share your toys."

Mama also taught me to never kiss and tell, so I decided to change the subject. I asked Lamar if he was going to share his notes with his playing partner of the day and he told me he would be glad to if the money was right. He didn't mind sharing them with me, mainly because we had both played in all ten Classics and even managed to win one each. Bubba came in third with eight years and one win under his belt. No one else had managed to stay around more than three years.

About half an hour later, Bubba managed to show up. At least it looked like Bubba and walked like Bubba, but the sunglasses snuggled darkly around his eyes hid his true identity.

We both acknowledged his presence as he plopped down in a metal folding chair across the table from us, but all we got in return was some sort of garbled message that sounded like a female buffalo in heat.

I told Bubba that it looked to me like old Jack Daniels had beat him in match-play and then asked him if he had his caddie paint his sticks white with a red tip on the heads yet, cause it looked to me like he was definitely going into this round blind.

"Son, I got me a whole head full of hurt this morning and I can hardly see out of this side of these old eyeballs of mine, but if you would care to wager, say a grand or so, that this here old man can't beat you on this here old course today, then you just say them words I dearly love to hear and we can cut out all the bullshit."

I told him I'd certainly like to take him up on his offer, but I didn't rightly enjoy taking money from friends. I much preferred robbing strangers. I told him that Kenny Winner had been in earlier and had headed out to the practice range and that he might ought to do the same. He proceeded to tell me that he had no intention of wasting his best shots where they didn't count. Said it was sort of like jackin' off, and he didn't do much of that either.

I left the tent about nine-thirty and made my usual stop at the clubhouse to see if Thumper needed anything. He seemed in a much better mood than when I left him yesterday evening. I didn't really feel the urge to continue our discussion about Kelly, so I made the first move at new conversation. "Well, which greens do I stay left of today?"

"All of 'em if you plan on winning." Although he knew what I meant, he obviously countered accordingly to make sure my head was still in the game.

I told him I had looked at Lamar's notes and saw that he was up to his usual tricks and that the course played hell-bent as it was without adding insult to injury. He told me that if I couldn't play with the big boys, I didn't have no business teeing off. I started to tell him that Lamar had commented that he made the greens harder than a whore's heart, but my mind quickly reminded me of last night, so I took a free drop from the comment.

I could see that I wasn't needed here, so I decided to go pick up my Footjoys and find my caddie. As I was about out the door, Thumper warned me to stay off the back of the Number 3 green. He mentioned that Miss Prize Tits, who I learned was one Denise Van Zant from over near Humble, had forgotten to take off her shoes in the heat of the moment. I thanked him for that important bit of information and left him to whatever it was he had been doing when I came in.

I stopped myself on the porch of the clubhouse and watched a now familiar figure as he walked across Whipoorwill and up the road to the tent. He grabbed what was now his usual one beer and headed to the Number 1 tee. I continued to stare for what seemed to be a full walk up a par 5 fairway, until Kelly Dale drove the full length of Number 1, this time stopping fifteen feet on the right front of the green.

It wasn't going to be anything but your routine birdie, if not an eagle. Dean Shillings was probably going to end up dead meat if he tried to keep up.

As I walked to the locker room, I kept reminding myself to just play my own game. It was the course I had to beat.

Adrian Hodges was in the locker room when I finally found my way there. I had me another young pup to raise, but at least I didn't have this one head on. Adrian had beaten his match-play opponent rather handily yesterday, which should have been no surprise. Out of all the newcomers, he had been weaned on a course similar, though not nearly as deadly as Cut N Shoot. His home course was the Buffalo Creek Golf Club in the Mark Twain National Forest of southern Missouri. I, myself, have never seen the course first hand, but Golf Digest ran a series of articles several years ago about the fifty hardest municipal courses in these United States, of which Buffalo Creek was number four. We all know which course sat at the top of the list, two votes shy of an acclamation. Anyhow, Buffalo Creek was carved directly into and out of solid rock. They had to bring dirt in to lay the fairways. The only difference between our two courses as far as the nut-cuttin' goes is ours is longer by at least a third.

We shared a word or two, sort of feeling each other out, then I asked him if he was ready to face my daddy's pride and joy, not me, the course, of course. He acknowledged in the affirmative and off we went.

Kenji Lee and Petey Nielsen, Hawaii and Kansas, respectively, had just plastered their drives near the front edge of the green. Kenji was to the right with a decent chance to chip close and putt for the bird, while Petey was to the left and in a shit-pot full of trouble with a bunker to fly and nowhere near the pin to land. Kenji had survived last year and was well aware of Thumper's evil ways.

Me and my playing partner managed routine birdies on Number 1, at which time I realized Adrian was not only a good golfer but also what we call visitor smart. He knew this was my home course, so he gave me the honors and then followed my drive, even so far as managing to get just inside me so that I would have to hit first again. It didn't take my feeble mind but one hole to see what he was up to, so on the next hole I faked a flub shot to the left and short, knowing he wouldn't dare follow suit on what would be considered a missed shot. Sure enough, he drove straight up the fairway on the dog-leg 599 yard horseshoe par 5, leaving himself one more shot to make the corner and another 250 yards to the green. If he could get on from that distance, which was doubtful, he would still have two putts to make par. And even a bogey wouldn't be so bad for the hardest hole on the course. Of course, what he hadn't expected was old Joe Don here, being the master of the power fade. From my far-left lie, I sliced a huge banana clean around both corners to the middle of the home stretch and laid my third shot to the front center of the green. Although it took me two more to get down, I carded your natural par, and as predicted, he came up short on his third, got on with his fourth and two-putted.

I was beating the course at its own game.

There were no tricks on Number 3, where you just prayed to be on with your first shot and accepted a two-putt as gravy.

I routinely bogeyed six of the next fifteen holes and settled for par on the others and finished at plus 5, which was good enough for a three-way tie for second with B.J. Littlejohn and my good buddy, Lamar. There was a two-way tie for the lead at plus 4. Adrian ended at plus 8, which wasn't quite good enough by a hair.

There were two at plus 4, three at plus 5, seven at plus 6, five at plus 7 and six at plus 8. The rest didn't matter. Only three in that last group of plus 8 would make the cut, which was decided as usual by going to the hardest handicap hole and working your way back up the scorecard. Adrian lost out at Number 9, where he took a double bogey.

It was no miracle that no one parred the course. No one has ever parred the course. One over par is the course record and that is held by a fellow by the name of Casey Grey from Arizona back in Classic VI. He also managed that score on a Friday, then managed a gut-wrenching plus 17 the following day and didn't make the final cut. Back then, when we weren't playing match-play the first day, we gave everyone a free ride on Thursday and then cut the troops down Friday and Saturday.

I and four others hold down second place on the course at plus 2 and I've only done that twice.

I was feeling pretty hospitable toward my score until I reached the leader board, where my body told me I needed to shit. I was glad I hadn't taken old Bubba up on his offer of a wager at breakfast. There he was, tied for the lead with a stroke advantage over me. What I wasn't so fucking glad about was who he was tied with. Young Mr. Dale had posted the other plus 4 and he was nowhere to be seen.

Thumper was standing by the board watching intently as Melanie worked the numbers as only she could do it, and refused to make eye contact with me.

I grabbed a warm scotch in a tall cup and sat down in the tent to watch as the other scores came wandering in. After the last one of the day was posted, I made my way back over to Cabin 12 for a cold shower and a little time for thought. I had played my heart out and carded what should have been an acceptable score, but my soul was tired.

I talked myself into believing that there were still two playing days left before falling into a restless sleep, naked on top of the bed.

* * *

I awoke to the presence of someone entering the room. Although still cloudy with sleep, I had an easy feeling that the intruder meant me no harm. Maybe it was the fact that this lovely shadow was undressed in the same attire as me. As her body became my cover, my exhausted soul was reborn, with no memory of the day passed.

By the time Melanie and I returned to the real world, it was half past eight. I felt an urgency to return to the course to see who I would be paired with tomorrow. It would either be Lamar or B.J., since we were bunched up together with the same score, 77. Bubba and

Kelly Dale would be paired as they shared the lead. My need passed almost as quickly, as Melanie could see the restlessness in my eyes and told me I had drawn my buddy Lamar. B.J. would be with Spook Taylor, one shot behind us.

She poured me a deep scotch as I dressed, pondering again on the game we are involved in. Not about today's happenings, but tomorrow's. My strength was returning in the realization that I had always played my best golf when Lamar and I shared the course. One of the two times I had shot two over was when I was playing with him. I also didn't mind none that Kelly would be playing with Bubba. After the way Bubba burned the course up today, I had a better than good mind to make sure he got teamed up, hot and heavy, with old Jack Daniels again tonight. Then I realized that old Bubba didn't need no help when it came to that twosome. He and Jack had been playing together for many a year.

Melanie, seeing that I had again entered a relaxed phase, strolled off into the shower. I left my Jaymars on the floor and strolled along behind her for what most golfers term as a shower for power. Even the worst duffer will tell you that power golf is played from the legs and there is no healthier, if not cleaner, way to build up the thigh muscles than to make love while standing belly-to-belly under warm, soapy water. Weightlifters and bodybuilders of the world got no idea what they are missing. A good woman and a warm shower beats the living shit out of a Nautilus machine any day of the week.

Since Friday nights at The Cut N Shoot Classic are reserved for your better-than-average time at The Crystal Pistol and since yours truly is supposed to be one of the hosts at this here yearly shindig, it was decided by a majority vote of two that we had better put any further training aside and make our presence known at that given location. Realizing that neither of us had taken the time to eat in the last eight hours or so, and that it would be a long spell until Lucy cranked up breakfast, we made a pit stop at Pooch's Pound on the way over. Pooch's menu consists of only three items: a half-pound burger, cheese and fries. And old Pooch only knows one way to cook 'em; well done. Now mind you, it wasn't as good as the hickory fajitas the other contestants had received at the mess tent on the course earlier, but when I considered what my appetizer had been, old Pooch's burger could just as well have been a T-bone steak with all the trimmings.

The Crystal Pistol in Cut N Shoot's hideaway. There ain't a town in Texas, or any other state for that matter, that doesn't have one. If someone tells you different, then either he's lying or he ain't looked hard enough. The Pistol, like almost every other establishment in this town, is also just off 105, only way off. We made the 2 ½ mile, caliche drive through the pines until we came in sight of the music. See, The Pistol is nothing more than a thousand or more square feet of screened porch, only the porch isn't attached to anything. To the perimeter of this overbuilt gazebo is attached probably a quarter of a mile of colored crystal lights tuned in to the stereo system so that the lights flash according to the music. The red lights are tuned to the deep base, blue to the lighter bass and on down the scale. So, when I said we saw the music, I meant just that. We **saw** the music.

No one knows or remembers where the pistol in Crystal Piston came from, but no one really cares. Once you enter this world of topless dancers, you ain't got but one thing on your solid mind anyway; tits and ass and all you can feast your eyes on.

As Melanie parked my VW on the outskirts of the lot, she pointed to the woods behind the screened building. As usual, there was a multitude of Cut N Shoot's younger sons perched on the heavier pine branches, trying to catch a glimpse of their future. Rita Fowler, the present owner, could make a decent living just by charging admission for those balcony seats alone. I smiled at myself as fond memories of younger Friday nights passed through my eyes. Thumper and I fell out of many a pine tree before reaching the age of consent.

The party was already in full swing, to say the least. Rita had herself parked on her usual stool by the door and gave Melanie an unsure eye as we approached. You see, Rita and Hazel had themselves what you would call a businesswoman's agreement. Neither one would cross over into the other one's turf. However, when she caught a glimpse of who was connected to the arm Melanie was clinging to, she relaxed and let her enter without a hassle. Not that I am any type of celebrity in these parts, but since I was footing the bill for the evening, it meant that this piece of bread was buttered on my side.

It didn't take long to see who the real party animals were. Bubba, although not on Rita's payroll, was on the stage amongst 'em, stripped to the waist, a bottle of Jack in one hand and the left rear quarter of one of the dancers in the other. He would be hell on the course tomorrow, thank goodness.

B.J., which honestly and truly stood for Big John, was sharing another spotlight, although still fully clothed. On his shoulders, facing in the opposite direction, mind you, was one of your more heavenly endowed ladies at probably eight to ten over par on our front nine. The only way I could tell the bottom half was B.J. was the fact that he was wearing scotch-plaid knickers, which no other decent living American would dare wear out in public. And besides, I had seen his dance routine before.

Some of the rookies were even joining in the sanctioned melee. Emmet "Dub" Cole of Michigan was down to his Fruit-of-the-Looms and attempting to keep time with the music with what looked to be a cluster-fuck rendition of the Twist-Dog-Swim-Monkey. He was being given a wide berth by the other participants cause any fool could see that he was there, but he wasn't; if you know what I mean. He obviously didn't make the cut.

Bradford Tillman of Vermont, who, by the way, **had** made the cut, was seriously into the evening. Brad, who stands maybe four foot eleven, five foot in his Footjoys, was completely void of his evening wear and perched on the shoulders of one of the stouter built ladies, looking contentedly like the blind hog who done found his acorn.

I made a mental note to myself to make sure I arrived at breakfast early enough to catch the morning acts of those who were giving their all so that the rest of us might thoroughly enjoy ourselves.

Melanie and I had been gone an hour when the lights went out at The Crystal Pistol, so we missed the last act of the evening. Chris Carmichael, being from Nevada and no stranger to this life form, talked Madam Rita onto the stage, flashing one of those green bills with a one followed by three zeros, proving everyone has a price. He neatly wrapped the bill around old John Henry and dared her to obtain the bill using nothing more than her dentures. Without going into further detail, let me just say that Rita woke up Saturday morning with a thousand-dollar bill tip on her nightstand.

And me, I woke up to play.

SHOOT, SKATE AND RATTLESNAKE STEAK

Although Melanie had set the alarm for seven sharp before we passed on into nothing more than restful sleep, I was rudely awakened by the chattering of two squirrels on a pine branch just outside the open window. They were going at each other like two hackers arguing over a gimme putt. The clock said I had but five minutes left, so I canceled the alarm in order to give my bed partner some extra beauty sleep, not that she needed it, mind you. My mind instantly centered itself on the day ahead. I was determined to go out and do nothing more than make up the one-stroke difference and let Sunday take care of the rest.

I quickly showered, alone this time, remembering that a treat awaited me at breakfast. Last night's revelers would definitely add a flavorful color to the morning meal. Melanie hadn't moved during my absence, so I agreed with myself to just let her sleep in. As my uniform of the day, I chose chocolate brown slacks and a cream-colored Hogan shirt with an April Sound emblem on the left sleeve. I had worn this same combination the last time I managed my two-over-par round on my home course. There was no reason for me to be any different than any other fifteen million superstitious Americans who play some four hundred and fifty million rounds on thirteen thousand golf courses each year. That many idiots can't be wrong.

I sat for a minute and watched Melanie's easy breathing before challenging the short walk to the course.

Once again, I found Lamar already seated and studying his notepad. I made my usual greetings in Lucy's direction and joined my old friend deep in thought.

"Just like old times, huh?" My question seemed to catch him off guard as he quickly closed the cover of his pad.

"What?" He seemed to be elsewhere for the moment.

"We're playing together. Or haven't you seen the board yet?" I went on to ask him if the fact that we were tied and going head-to-head meant that I had joined the ranks of those who would have to pay to see his scribblings on what old Thumper had managed to do to see that none of us would particularly enjoy the game once we got to the greens.

"No, no! I just didn't expect you to be you."

"Really? Who did you expect me to be, Mary Queen of Fucking Scots?"

Without aiming, he fired his pad directly at me, wounding my Styrofoam coffee cup and dripping its pale brown blood across my right hand. "Oops, sorry."

"Hey, no problem. I just use that hand to guide with anyway."

I picked the small paper booklet off the ground and plopped it back on the table between us and asked him if there was any interesting reading between the lines.

"Son, either you gotta have a talk with Thumper or we gotta get an early call in to K-Mart and have them send us over a truckload of Vaseline. The man's done gone crazy on us."

I flipped open the pad and finger-ran through the pages until I located what looked to be today's date scrawled at the top of one of the pages. I grinned inside as I waded through the notes. It wasn't so much that Thumper had moved the cups back, but he had terrorized them by setting them on the back slopes. This meant nothing more than an uphill to downhill putt from the front or an arcing sidehill one from the left or right. If we tried to approach past the hole for an acceptable downhill putt, chances are we would be putting from off the green.

I tried to make light of the situation and reminded him that it wasn't anything we hadn't seen before and that we should be thankful that old Thump at least left the cups on the putting surface. He just shook his head as I handed him back his closely guarded secret. As the other golfers began to arrive, he stuffed his tablet into his back pants pocket so as not to give anything away.

My planned early arrival had not gone for naught. The first wave of newcomers entered, laughing beyond control and holding their heads with each gasp. They were followed by a limping Chris Carmichael, who approached the tent with the moves of one who looked like he had just had a corn cob shoved deep into the recesses of his posterior. It was then that I was made aware of the final event at The Pistol last night, or should I say earlier this morning. It was hard to determine whether the pain on his face was from the injury to his organ or to his wallet.

B.J. slithered in smelling of Listerine and looking like someone had taken a Brillo pad to the lower part of his face. When Bryant Paschall of Iowa mentioned AIDS in B.J.'s direction, he quickly exited stage left and ran to the clubhouse for further minor antiseptic surgery.

Little Bradford Tillman didn't look the worse for wear, although his gait rocked along somewhat dizzily, possibly from the heights he had achieved the previous evening.

Dub Cole was a no-show, and when questioned, none of the others could say for certain that they ever saw him leave. Rira did assure me later that he was delivered safe, though unsound, to his cabin. She had even allowed one of her girls to stay with him to make sure he continued to breathe on a regular basis. That, in itself, could be one reason for his absence.

Now, Bubba was another story. He arrived, sans sunglasses, and yelling that he was hungry enough to eat a herd of buffalo. He quickly apologized needlessly to Lucy, telling her that he surely wasn't comparing her delicious feast to that particular species of animal as he piled up triple portions of everything onto two plates. As usual, she smiled from behind her Winston.

He lumbered on over to where me and Lamar were relaxing over not-so-mountainous meals and announced that he was ready to tackle whatever this old course had to offer him today.

I wasn't so sure that I liked his particular attitude this morning. Speaking from experience and as any fairly good linkster knows, even the best feelings about this here old game can be quickly shattered by one errant shot. It's a sad but true fact that many a good game is shot by one under the weather, so to speak, than by one who has set his sights high before teeing off, only to fall off that mountain early on and never regain his footing.

"I don't know how you do it, Bubba. I could have sworn on my daddy's grave that your sweet ass would be dragging this morning."

"Son, you just gotta teach your body who's boss, that's all."

I reminded Bubba that the last time I saw his body, it was stripped to the waist and attempting to tango with Brother Jack and some bare-assed young thing with enormous mammaries. He reminded me that this old life ain't nothing but a game, and if you don't get in there and play that old game, then it'll turn you around and play you. He went on to say that the game of golf wasn't no different and that he had every intention of going out there today and opening up a mean can of whip-ass and pouring it all over this little old course of mine.

For me, I sure as hell hoped he was right. Matter of fact, I think I even told him so.

★ ★ ★

I knew not to waste mt time looking for the other co-leader; however, the thought struck me to have the beer keg moved to another location out of sight in order to maybe screw up his obvious pre-game ritual. The host in me, however, won that match.

I followed my own ritual and sought out Thumper in his usual morning lair. I hadn't talked to him since the previous morning and knew from his lack of geniality after my round yesterday that I would probably be less than welcome this morning. However, we both had our jobs to do and right now mine was to see how his was coming along.

This morning, he was standing on the clubhouse porch, surveying his handiwork from afar. To my surprise, he made the first move toward conversation. "You feel better than five over today, sport?"

"Matter of fact, I do. But you ain't exactly helping my game by adding to my putting percentage." I thought I would ease whatever tension might be present by acknowledging his efforts at strengthening the course.

"I didn't change nine." That was one of his stock answers, since the Number 9 pin couldn't be moved more than two feet in any direction. That little bitty green just happens to have a four-sided slope and any pin placement much past dead center would give the golfer an unplayable lie anywhere on the green. My daddy said when he built this course, that all courses should have at least one silly hole and this one was it. If you don't believe what I'm telling you, you can always go ask Sandy Sanders, who has firsthand knowledge of the landscape.

I thanked him for his small favor and followed by asking if Denise had added any of her own little hazards to our course. To that, he replied that I should beware of the claw marks on the front of Number 13 green. Seems as though they were trying a new position at that spot and he damn near lost her to the crevasse below. I asked him if she was the kind of girl who got her thrills by living on the edge, and if so, anything she did after our little tournament was over would surely be a letdown compared to what he had lovingly exposed her to.

Thumper just smilingly shook his head. From there, we got back to the task at hand. "The way I see it, you ain't near out of this thing yet."

I agreed and told him about my plan to just go out there today and get myself even with Mr. Dale and let the chips fall where they may come tomorrow. For once, he agreed with me.

"And just remember, the greens are the course," I told him that nobody knew that better than him, and with that, he retired on back into the clubhouse, probably to think up some new and dishonest way to make the greens even more fatal for tomorrow's final round. It wouldn't surprise me none if he was in there right now praying to the golf god to send down a night full of hundred-mile-an-hour winds to dry the greens out so much, they'd be faster than a fart on a hot skillet. At least my subconscious hadn't yet lost its sense of humor.

I still had about two hours left before my round was scheduled to start, but I was already itching to get out there. I found my bag and latched hold of my short irons and headed for the practice range. Thumper had made one-putting almost next to impossible, but a little practice on getting close wouldn't hurt matters none.

Upon arriving, I found Lamar had the same idea as me, so we spent the next hour aiming and betting. Nothing heavy, mind you, but still a little heavier than kisses and fucks.

We would have probably spent a little longer mastering our skills had not two familiar faces taken the liberty of interrupting our little game. Old Number 99, Billy Ray Breedlove, with Brucie in tow, were making their way about the course, getting ready for their next scheduled appearance later in the day. A third face was hidden behind a shoulder-mounted mini-cam, ready to record our little impromptu get-together for posterity.

"You boys just never quit, do you?" Billy Ray called out as they arrived at their destination. The cameraman was already easing his trigger finger onto the record button.

Since we still had some time to kill, I thought I would give our two less-than-expert commentators a few words of wit and wisdom I had picked up over the years, mostly from watching the game on TV. I figured it was the least I could do to keep the telecast from being void of any authentic words on golf mania. I had no doubt that Lamar would follow suit.

I started out by introducing Lamar to our two celebrities and telling them that he'd been hitting the woods pretty well here of late, but he was having one hell of a time getting out of them. Billy Ray, part-time golfer that he was, understood the pun; however, it went right directly over old Brucie's head.

Lamar countered by saying that I played in the low eighties, and that if it got any hotter, I just wouldn't play. Before I could add further to the conversation, Brucie jumped in, again not understanding the comment, and said that it was supposed to be ninety degrees in the shade today. I got him off the hook by explaining that that wouldn't bother us too much cause we didn't play in the shade.

With the camera still rolling, Billy Ray mentioned that the course seemed to be overloaded with bunkers and wondered if that gave me too much trouble. I told him that I was in the bunkers so much yesterday that my caddie got blisters on his hands from raking so much. Lamar took up where I left off and mentioned that he had been in more bunkers here than Eva Braun.

Brucie again tried to join in the game and asked if the greens were giving us any trouble. Now, what this meant was that they had stopped in to see Thumper before heading out onto the course. Lamar jumped in first and told him that not only are three-putt greens probable, but at times they are an achievement. I then gave them a quote they probably wouldn't be able to use on TV and told them putting on old Thumper's greens was like putting on titties. Not to be outdone, Lamar added that the way the pins were set yesterday, he worried his second putt before he even hit the first one.

We figured we had used up enough clichés on that subject, so we both shut up and waited for the next. Billy Ray brought up the matter of the length of the course and how it was probably twice as long as most of the ones he had played. Lamar agreed with him and pointed out that by the time he had gotten to his ball on Number 16 yesterday, he was too tired to hit it. I started to say that they ought to hang the man who designed the course, until I remembered just who that was; so I just said that most of the par threes here were long par fours on other courses.

Realizing that we needed to be getting back to the clubhouse and on to our scheduled appointment at Number 1, I asked them if there was anything else about this silly game that they thought their viewers would like to know. Brucie, out of character, was speechless and Billy Ray just sort of stood there waiting for me to continue, so I did.

"Well, fellas, all I can say about this here old game is that it's sorta like a love affair. If you don't take it seriously, it ain't no fun. And if you do take it seriously, it'll break your heart."

Again, not to be outdone. Lamar added his own, or someone else's, bit of advice. He said, "Golf is like fishing or hunting. What counts is the companionship, not what you catch or shoot."

With those words, we left those two with their own thoughts to ponder, and once they were out of earshot, I told him that if he really believed that last piece of advice, then I guess he didn't really want the fifty bucks he'd won on our chipping contest out there on the practice range.

⋆⋆⋆

Blake Quantrell and Donald "Pigeon" Towze, from that Buckeye State of Ohio, teed off in front of B.J. and Spook. Now, Pigeon didn't get that nickname because he was an easy mark on the links. It just so happens that his feet are cross-eyed, which isn't exactly a bad break for a golfer. With his awkward stance, he couldn't slice the ball even if he had a mind to. However, he did get your maximum roll from his name, especially when playing a new course where his skills had not yet preceded him. He and his usual playing partner and college roommate, Linwood Borowitz, would simply arrive at a chosen course as a twosome, whereupon they would ask to be paired with any unsuspecting members. After the usual introductions, where his name would be taken for its obvious face value by their newly acquainted and gullible playing partners, Linwood and Pigeon would throw the first two or three holes. It never failed that the members would then make their fatal move and ask if wagers might be in order. From then on, the member lambs were led to slaughter-city. They never had too much of a problem in collecting on their bets, as golfers for the most part understand that once you tee it up and slap that first one down the fairway, it's open season on everybody and everything. On those few times where it looked like their collection may be in jeopardy, they simply reminded the actual pigeons of who it was that requested wagers be the order of the day in the first place.

Blake, whose golf stance resembles a monkey fucking a football, and Pigeon both spanked your better-than-average drive; however, Thumper had made sure that routine for this hole today would be par, not birdie.

B.J. and Spook followed as we prepared for out eighteen-hole journey. We waited until they had putted out before starting. With only ten pairs playing today, there would be no rush. Before hitting, I glanced back toward the tent, hoping to find the final twosome of the day heading our way. I wanted the young Mr. Dale to catch a glimpse of what he had in store for himself today at my expense. But I saw only disappointment. He would, no doubt, make his usual last-minute entrance with no time to spare.

Again, thanks in part to my buddy, Thumper, me and Lamar also settled for today's customary par on Number 1. As I placed the flag back in the cup, I glanced back up the fairway in time to see Kelly stepping up onto the tee box. Since he obviously hadn't seen our play on the hole, I held up three fingers and hoped Father Psyche would do the rest.

Lamar, not being privy to my actual task at hand, thought I was trying to get Bubba riled up. "Shit, Joe Don! Bubba's good enough to wax our combined asses without you giving him something to shoot for."

I played along with his misguided hunch and told him that old Bubba was going to need all the help he could get, cause I was about to bring Daddy's course to its knees. He responded by reminding me that compared to yesterday's score on the previous hole, I was one stroke off the pace. And damn him if he wasn't correct.

We both bogeyed Number 2, then settled back into your basic par playing until we reached Number 8, the third par 5 on the front nine. Lamar tried to drive the second cut on this double dog-leg with a two wood second shot, but found the water on the far side and had to accept a double bogey. I tried to play it safe, but entered the sand that surrounds the green in three. I did manage to get out with my next shot, but was left with a forty-two footer, which I managed to break up in two shots. I was now one up on Lamar, but two over for the round at this point. It wasn't hard for me to understand that I would have to par in if I was going to match my own second-place course record.

We hit the Number 9 green just as the cameras started into action. I wondered if Big Billy Ray had led off the verbal action with any of his newfound quotes on this asinine little game we all hate to love. After I hit my shot to the green directly below us, a soft sand wedge that hit the up-slope of the front and refused to bounce, I thought of another bit of golf humor I must have heard while watching the pros go at it one Sunday afternoon in the not-so-distant past. At the moment, I cannot remember the characters involved, but one of the all-time money winners had just hit a beautiful approach shot to the green, to which one of the announcers commented:

"So and so sure has a smooth touch."

This was followed by the obvious color announcer's reply:

"Yeah. As smooth as a man lifting a breast out of an evening gown."

I was kinda sorry I hadn't remembered that one back on the practice range. It surely would have been usable material.

We settled for routine pars and tipped our caps to the audience nestled around the green. B.J. and Spook were just now teeing off at 10, so we paused for a quick scotch to settle the ever-present yips. Lamar said he felt a small hunger pang, so he grabbed himself a cold chicken leg and chewed around it. I reminded him that he might ought to wash his hands when he was through, as I sure would hate for the viewing audience to see his Muirfield driver squirting up the fairway ahead of his ball.

As we made our way back to business, the crowd around the 9th green let out a gasping scream. We detoured over their way and found an obvious birdie in the making. Either Bubba or young Kelly had obviously found a smoother breast than mine, cause there was a little white orb sitting up not four inches from the pin and shining in the early afternoon sun like a diamond in a goat's ass. There was no way in hell I was going to leave this spot until I found out who the owner of that shot was.

The next player wasn't so lucky as the sand behind the green resounded with a gut-wrenching thump.

As Kelly and Bubby rounded the side of the cliff and headed for the natural green carpet, all doubt as to who the culprit was was put to a final rest. Bubba's caddie was handing him a sand wedge.

I turned and headed to Number 10, not wanting to view first-hand the obvious outcome. Masochism was not on my Top 10 list of vices.

We played down Number 10 and up Number 11 in par. At Number 12, a one hundred and fifty yard, par 3 straight uphill, Lamar began feeling the adverse effects of his chicken leg. His tee shot hit the front of the bunker and shot straight up in the hot air. As the ball came down, it kicked back off the bunker and rolled straight back downhill. And Lamar threw up. His only saving grace was that the cameras were focused on yesterday's leaders behind us.

I only fared slightly better from the tee, ending in the sand on the back. The golf god, however, was smiling down on big old me. My shot from the sand hit the flagstick, stopping dead in its tracks about the same distance from the cup as Kelly's had on Number 9.

I tapped in a par and Lamar took a double. It was turning out to be obvious as to who I would be playing with and against in tomorrow's final round. The only question left to be answered was how many strokes down I would be when we began.

Lamar never quite got back into the hunt, and me, I managed to save par on all the remaining holes with the exception of Number 17. Sixteen and seventeen are your unbasic, 600 yard, uphill tiered par fives. My middle-aged bones just plain wore out. It took me three whole strokes just to manage the second tier and once on, I again split a forty-plus putt into two slaps. Bogey number three.

I posted a three over 75 and Lamar managed to break 80 by one stroke, and swore off fried chicken legs for life. I really had no desire to hang around and be a glutton for punishment. My mind was on a lukewarm shower and whatever else might present herself. I could read the final results of today's rounds on the leaderboard later.

As I was about to head for Cabin 12, I was approached by one of the KHSN flunkies and asked to join Billy Ray and Brucie on the tower. Host that I was, or at least needed to be, I accepted. No sooner had I set foot on the platform high above 18 than Billy Ray was shaking my hand and slapping a headset on me and asking how it felt to almost be tied for the lead.

For once in my not-so-young life, I was totally speechless. A faceless man in the TV panel control truck parked in the parking lot was telling me through the headset that Kelly Dale was putting a fifty-six-footer for a natural bogey on 18, and a two put would give him a 76 for the day. It didn't take no mathematician to figure out that his 76-76-152 would come face to face with my 77-75-152. I suddenly wished I had been given a chance to pee before being summoned up here.

My partner for tomorrow gave it his best shot and one that would make even the loosest sphincter muscle pucker. His ball came to rest no more than half a revolution from the cup for an inherent double bogey, and no tip of the cap.

I still had no earthly idea what happened and just sat there, fully head-setted like an unplayable lie. With only five minutes left in the telecast, I decided to remain calm and, above all, keep my mouth shut until I found out the meaning of life as it pertained to today's round. The faceless man in the truck switched my headset from his mike to Billy Ray's so I could hear the final wrap-up. I got there in just enough time to hear old number 99 comment something about Kelly's caddie having to rake so much sand on Number 18 that he had blisters on his hands. I looked over at this bulk of a man wearing a grin from ear to ear and winked. And from the expression on old Brucie's face, it was evident that he still didn't get the punchline.

When the headset went dead, I finally had a chance to question Billy Ray about the whys and wherefores of my sudden fortune. He proceeded to explain to me in detail how my co-leader, who was minus one for the front nine, had rolled his tee shot off the back of the par 3 Number 15 green and settled for a bogey; following that up with back to back bogeys on 16 and 17, before going completely to pieces on 18, hitting the left sand, then the right sand, then the left sand again. If that wasn't bad enough, he then proceeded to hit his fourth shot of the par 5 into yet more sand to the back of the green. From there, he over-blasted back down to the front of the green. I thanked him and told him that I knew what happened after that.

With a complete understanding of the action behind me now, I was able to provide the two commentators with a short, taped interview, which they promised would be shown on the 10 O'clock News.

I provided them with a final bit of golf lore to end the interview by reminding them of what the late and great Bobby Jones once said.

"If you keep shooting par at them, they all crack sooner or   later."

I left the course looking even more forward to my lukewarm shower and whatever.

✳ ✳ ✳

It wasn't until running a steady stream of tepid water over my body that I came to realize how thoroughly exhausted I actually was. To my surprise, I was also actually thankful that Melanie had chosen to stay at the course and help Hazel with the last-minute planning of the after-hours social event scheduled for Patsy's Roller Dome and Bingo Hall.

As superstitiously usual, I reclined naked on top of the bed; however, sleep was apparently not on the agenda. I replayed each shot of today's round in my head and then went back to yesterday's. I tried counting golf balls as they sailed over front bunkers and next to the pin for gimmes. I got up and poured myself a heavy scotch, hoping to dull my senses into at least a par 3 nap, but the course was playing long. I even reversed my earlier gratitude and hoped Melanie **would** see fit to grace my rustic surroundings with her presence. But she didn't.

Accepting my fate, I got up and dressed in faded Levi's and a midnight blue Cut N Shoot Golf Club shirt and wandered back on over to the scene of today's crime. The crowd had thinned out considerably, so I grabbed a second scotch and walked over to the leader board to make sure it hadn't all been some sort of wicked dream. It wasn't. There in front of my eyes were the standings.

79

             DALE, K   76-76-152

             BUGGS, J   77-75-152

             TAYLOR, S   78-75-153

It was the third score that caught my eye. I had been worrying so much about beating Kelly Dale that I let all the other players escape. When a golfer does that, it is a sure sign that his old ass is about to be hung out to dry. Thumper had warned me about Spook Taylor, or at least tried to, but as usual, my mind was in neutral. The boy had done gone out today and almost matched my round, hole by hole. B.J. Littlejohn was also to be reckoned with in fourth place on the board with a solid 154. They had obviously complemented each other's play.

I was so thoroughly involved with the numbers that I failed to hear Thumper come up behind me. "Not a record, but it'll do in a pinch."

He caught me completely off-guard, causing me to spill my yet untouched scotch all over my lizard-skin Tony Lamas. "Shit, Thump! Don't you believe in giving a guy some warning/"

I cleaned my boots on the back of my jeans and made a mental note to give them to my caddie to clean later. Alcohol and lizard can cause about as much damage as alcohol and driving.

"From the looks of the board up there, you better be keepin' a closer watch on your backside." He obviously hadn't been reading my mind or he would have known his comment was unnecessary.

It wouldn't have done much good to brag on the fact that I had gone out and done what I set out to do and that was to get myself into a winning position. But I did it anyway. He went on to tell me that it was none of my doing. I hadn't got myself in a tie with Kelly, the course had. The course beat Kelly today, not me. I went on to realize that I should have gone with my first thought and kept my mouth shut.

"I guess tomorrow you'll go out and try to beat the kid head-to-head?" He was baiting me and I knew it. What's more, I wasn't going to bite.

"Nope." That was all I needed to say on the subject. I surely didn't need one of Thumper's sermons on playing the course and not the player. Once a day was more than enough.

"Good." With that reply, Thumper adjourned to the bar, grabbed a Lone Star from the cooler and left me alone.

There would be no aroma about the tent tonight as Stumpy would be cooking up the grub at his place and trucking it over to Patsy's later. I drained my half-empty scotch and then thought about a refill, not one of my harder decisions of the day. I filled my glass only three-quarters full this round in case there might be others lurking in the afternoon shadows, preparing to attack my unsuspecting backside.

I thought about chasing after Thumper to see if he might like some help in getting the new pin placements down early, but then I remembered he had his routine the same as all of us and he didn't need me interrupting his schedule. I was also no match for Denise in the tit category, so the very least I could expect from my offer would be a refusal.

I even considered checking with Smokey to see where young Mr. Dale was holed up and paying him an unexpected visit, but I reconsidered after realizing that four grueling hours tomorrow would be enough.

I knew I didn't want to return to my cabin and just sit and my mind still had no hankering for sleep. I took another long sip of scotch and had almost decided to go on over to the clubhouse and see what reruns were available when I caught a glimpse of a familiar figure making his way across Whirlpool.

The makeshift bar was blocking his view of my presence, but from my vantage point, I was able to watch him as he entered the locker rooms, then exited almost as quickly, his full bag of clubs slung across his shoulder. He rounded the building like a cat after a grounded bird and headed toward the practice range. It didn't take anyone no smarter than me to figure out where Kelly Dale had slipped off to on those late afternoons while the rest of us were deep in the party.

I gave him enough time to reach his destination and begin his work, then I followed. The practice range, same as the entire course, was surrounded by your ever-present pine trees. To the back left of the range, a small grove of yaupon was growing wild and this thick forest of skinny trees provided me sufficient cover no experienced spy would refuse to accept. I settled down beneath the growth about ten feet from the clearing.

I watched drive after drive clear the 250 yard marker dead center in the fairway on the fly. He then went to his long irons with the same consistency. I looked at my watch as I stood up to work the kinks out of my back and noticed that he had been at it for almost an hour, and had yet to give up.

He worked his way down his bag until he reached his 8 iron. I settled back down in a crouched position as he took aim at the green 150 yards out. His first shot hit the sand in front of the green, followed by a second in the trap to the left. I figured he was tired cause I damn sure knew I would be. His third hit the back bunker and his fourth, the trap on the right. I was almost feeling sorry for the kid until he put the next one on the green about a foot from the flag. He followed the same pattern with his next five shots and then did it a third time. The son of a bitch was doing it on purpose.

I watched him go through the same monotonous routine for fifteen more balls, then he grabbed his sand wedge and walked toward the green. From there, he played each and every shot from the sand to no more than five feet from the stick, sinking three for good measure. He retrieved all thirty balls and completely circled the outer edge of the green with them. He began putting from distances between thirty and fifty feet and sank more than he missed. He only broke stride when he had to go empty the loaded cup so he could refill it again.

The kid wasn't a golfer; he was a machine. A mother fucking golf machine. And I had to play with him tomorrow.

As he walked the range to pick up his solidly placed shots, the thought crossed my mind that maybe, just maybe, he had thrown the round today. He had finished poorly for no other reason than to be tied with me going into the final round. I cleanly forgot about Spook Taylor. There wasn't room for both of them in my mind's town.

I waited until he had left the range before even trying to stand, and then took a good five minutes to stretch my body back into shape before following his trail. As I neared the clubhouse, I saw him cross Whipoorwill and lose himself in the pines. I made my way back to the tent, as a heavy scotch was definitely prescribed by this doctor.

I thought about possibly practicing myself, but thank the golf god, the sun was near setting. It would have only made matters worse, me trying to follow his lead and failing.

Instead, I returned to Cabin 12 and allowed myself a second shower. Kelly Dale had been the one practicing, but I was the one sweating.

*　*　*

Melanie returned to pick me up a little before nine. She could tell my mind wasn't on the game she had planned, so we just said our hellos, jumped in her car this time and headed for Patsy's out on the loop.

We looked to be the last to arrive as everyone else was chowing down on what Stumpy was calling his rattlesnake steak. He managed a friendly, knowing grin as he heaped my plate full of the grayish-brown meat, cut thin and long. I sought out a table partially filled with newcomers for some fun and games. See, I knew our meal was nothing more than heavily seasoned and finely sautéed round steak, but the rookies didn't.

"Which do you boys prefer, the male or the female pieces?" They all stopped chewing in unison except for Gary Pollard of North Carolina, who almost choked trying to get his half-chewed portion down his throat.

Sam Werlinger of New York bit at my baited hook with the standard question of how to tell the difference. I went on to explain to this table of open ears that the darker gray meat was the male and the lighter, the female. I then asked them if they had noticed that the darker meat was more tender. Of course, they all shook their heads in the affirmative; all lies to the man. I let Melanie take over from there.

"See, boys, the female rattler produces about twenty or thirty little baby rattlers each spring, and unlike us human females, this causes her tummy to tighten up and makes the meat tougher." She then forked a piece of the darker meat and proceeded to chew easily. I looked around the table of new believers and could almost see their lips move as they counted her chews. She followed by taking in a piece of the lighter meat and went through the false routine of chomping down hard to mangle the meat enough to swallow.

After our little skit was over, we watched as our group picked up each bite and looked it over, trying to determine its gender before sending it home.

Stumpy often played that little trick at his own place of business. He had him a dozen menus printed up that looked just like the regular ones, with the exception of the added item under the Steak caption. When an unsuspecting diner who had never graced his establishment before entered, he pulled out one of those false menus and went to town. If you just happened to be dining there as one of his regulars, you were in for a rare treat at the expense of the unknowing guest.

It had been Bubba's idea for Stumpy to extend his joke to our little feast and ever since, we played it to the absolute hilt.

For this evening's affair, Patsy had divided the rink into two sections. One for dancing and one for skating. In place of her usual skating rink music, she had taped the Top 40 from last week's picks off her FM oldie station on the stereo in the back. We're talking groups that I ain't never heard of, much less danced to.

Nevertheless, Melanie was not about to let me sit out the evening, nor were any of Hazel's girls. It was either dance or skate. Sort of like, "Here's your drink, mister. Drink it or wear it."

Everyone danced. Everyone skated. And yes, everyone drank. Some of the old-timers, like Bubba, Lamar and B.J. had remembered the event from years passed and had obviously practiced. They began challenging the young ones to your usual skating contests, such as Crack the Whip, Loop the Loop, and even a new one, B.J. had brought with him from Arizona, called Smack the Twat.

Now, this latter event is not the kind you will usually find at your local rink and especially those places that cater to your church-function crowd. However, for the five days that our invitees are taking part in The Classic, all sins are forgiven. Me and the rest are not like this for the full 365; honest. Cut N Shoot is just like any other town in these here United States. The kids go to school on a regular basis. The neighbors are friendly. No one covets his neighbor's wife any more than they do anywhere else. The churches are always open. They got your better-than-average Fire and Police Departments and trash is picked up every Monday or Thursday, depending on your location. It's just that for five days every June, they let old Thumper take over. If I had kids of my own, that I knew about, I'd bring 'em up right here, just like I was.

But none of that has anything to do with B.J.'s game. For this event, each player is paired with a **willing** member of the opposite sex, which tonight is either one of Hazel's girls or some strange. The players take a practice round and skate together around the rink to make sure they got their sea legs, then pair by pair they start around the rink, girl partner in front. Halfway around the dome, the girl spreads her legs as far as humanly possible and her partner attempts to skate between her legs and lay a kiss on her underneath part before continuing to the front. The female partner could not help in any way.

It wasn't long before we all found out that it wasn't as easy as it was introduced and, in fact, no one, even B.J., could master the move. The trophy went back into the box.

From then on, the party livened quickly as everyone practiced old B.J.'s game in preparation for next year. As it turned out, it would be the same as at Cut N Shoot. This would be their one practice round, as I doubted seriously that their home rinks would sanction such an event. And, if they had a big enough driveway at home to practice on, they would have a heap of explaining to do to the little woman about where they picked up such an event and why they needed to practice.

Anyway, the game took on new meaning as the dance floor was cleared to extend the length of the rink. Partners swapped positions, bets were won and lost and trains were formed to see who could catch the most kisses before derailing all the cars.

Good old Bubba didn't fail at being the hit of the evening, as usual. When his turn came to pass under the female tunnel, he got as far as number three before losing his balance and falling backward, taking Paula Fay down with him. She landed smack on his face, rendering him senseless for a good two minutes. We all crowded around our fallen comrade and waited to see whether an ambulance should be summoned.

Bubba awoke with a start and looked Paula Fay straight in the eye and said, "Darlin', as long as I got me a face, you got yourself a place to sit."

The game sort of wound down from there as the vast majority of the players realized that they wouldn't be around for the event next year anyway and there was no sense going home injured and trying to explain how they could have possibly been wounded on the golf course.

Even the most golf-naïve wife knows it's a non-contact sport.

Half the rink was again roped off as most everyone commenced dancing or drinking, or dancing and drinking. It was nothing more than your natural high. See, I did have me this gentleman's agreement with Sheriff Zach Swift about not allowing any type of non-prescription drugs either on the course or at any of the related functions. That didn't bother me none. I didn't use the stuff and I didn't particularly care to be around those who did.

Around the end of the evening, Patsy returned us to the usual rink music and everyone more or less got back in touch with their natural, human emotions, guilt not being one. The last hour was nothing but belly to belly on the dance floor. Not a soul left until Patsy turned off the music and turned out the lights.

Either the evening or the scotch or both had taken my mind off what I had seen on the practice range earlier in the evening, but as we turned onto Whipoorwill, the memory returned with a passion. I felt a pain in the pit of my stomach and knew immediately it wasn't the scotch. Melanie picked up on my behavior as I stared blankly into the dark night in the direction of the course. She never uttered a word, even as we walked to the cabin, but once inside, she went directly to the closet and took out the same blanket we had been so fond of two nights ago.

I followed her out the door and leaned against a tall pine as she spread the cloth on the pine needle floor and began undressing, silhouetted by the pale-yellow light of the moon. I quickly followed her lead.

As we fell naked into an embrace, the same clouds that passed in front of the moon passed through my mind and erased my earlier memory.

Once again, we fell into a deep sleep. There was no rain to wake us this night as we slept till dawn, clinging to each other subconsciously for warmth.

I carried her inside and reset the alarm for nine.

TEE OFF AND TURN OUT THE LIGHTS

I clearly remember the first time I played golf with Bubba. I don't actually recollect which Classic it was, but I recall walking up onto the Number 1 tee box and having this meaty, worn hand stuck in my face. As I took his hand and looked at this man who was as big as a train wreck and twice as ugly, he said, "Son, I hope you've given your heart to your best girl and your soul to the Lord, cause your money and your ass are mine!"

That fond memory crossed my mind as I casually walked over to the mess tent for a mid-morning breakfast. It must have been the Lord part that brought about the recollection, since breakfast would be followed by a non-denominational church service, once the remains of the morning meal were clear away.

This was the one and only request that Mama made of me and Thumper. And we never turned down Mama's requests, after all, she was footing the bill for this shindig. Besides, we both love the hell out of that woman. Thumper especially, since both his parents and little brother, Cy, had been killed in a car accident over near Navasota when we were juniors in high school. Mama took him in just like he belonged, and when I think about it, I guess he did. She also added an addendum to her one request, and that was for me and Thumper to be in attendance.

She never asked us afterwards if we had attended, so we assumed she trusted us. What we found out later was that the preacher or priest, depending on who was asked to deliver the sermon, would report back to her that very afternoon on not only how many had attended but also whether her two lost sheep were accounted for.

Today's message was to be delivered by Pastor Raymond Crowder from the Light Baptist Church over in Groceville.

Lucy and her Winston were at their regular stations and presented me with their usual morning smile as I took a double portion of biscuits and sausage gravy. I looked around for a familiar face, but my usual cronies were either still asleep or had done come and gone, so I chose one of the smaller card tables near the edge of the tent and accepted my fate to eat alone.

Fate turned out to be kind, however. Just as my mind began to wander back to yesterday evening, I caught a glimpse of the ever-dependable Lamar walking off the 18th green, notebook in hand. As he ambled over toward the tent, I thought I caught a feint smile curling about his lips. As he drew closer, the smile broadened, leading me to believe that he must have gone off the deep end. After what Thumper had probably done to the pins for the main event, there should be no joy painted on any of our faces.

He plopped his pad on the square table and hurried over to the coffee urn to fill his cup. I found myself too afraid to pick the book up and read, so it just lay there like a lost ball in deep rough. I knew Lamar would fill me in on his return.

"Shit, son! Ain't you even gonna look?" Lamar questioned as he sat down across from me, needlessly warming his hands around the styrofoam cup.

"I think I'd rather hear it from your learned lips." I polished off the final swirl of peppered gravy with a crust of biscuit and waited.

He turned the small tablet toward me and flipped through the pages to one marked Sunday. From there, he turned page after page of what looked to me to be nothing more than the same page, over and over.

"Well, what do you see?" He seemed almost giddy in his hurried speech.

I told him his artwork left much to be desired, but with a little practice, he might get good enough to hang some on his refrigerator door.

"No, shithead! Look at this!" He went on to explain that the circles I saw with the dot in the middle of each were the actual center areas of the greens. The dot on each represented the hole.

I grabbed the book from him and flipped through it in disbelief. If what Lamar was showing me was true, and I had no reason I could think of at the moment to believe otherwise, then Thumper had actually gone out and stuck the pins directly in the center of each and every green. My buddy had actually made the course playable for me and the rest of the boys.

All I could do was look at Lamar and shake my head, and I think I may have even smiled. In ten years, I had seen old Thumper do this on only one other occasion, and that was for the final round of Classic VI. Thumper's reasoning for that move was due to the fact that we had us a four-way tie with a pair of right-handers and another pair who hit from the wrong side of the ball. He wanted to make sure the greens were fair to all the players. He said that if he put too many to the right or left, then it might possibly give an unfair advantage to two of the four. At that time, I told him he could have split it up and put an equal amount on each side. He advised me in no uncertain terms that I, as a fair golfer, should know that the holes are handicapped and even the slightest screw-up on his part by putting just two higher handicap hole pins to either side could be considered somewhat less than impartial. So, he just stuck them all in the middle and let the players fight it out.

I had no idea what his reasoning was today, but I was sure going to find out.

The tent began semi-filling up as the remnants of breakfast passed were cleared away. By the time Pastor Crowder stepped up to the make-shift pulpit, the place was packed. We're talking standing room only. During the opening prayer, which was offered by Jubal Washington, I caught a glimpse of the pastor taking his headcount for Mama and grinned to myself.

As usual, it wasn't your fire and brimstone sermon, but it did allow each of us the time needed to relax and ponder just what this old life really meant. The reverend ended, as always, with a prayer.

"And Lord, give these men the strength
to know Thy will and the accuracy to
keep their balls in the fairway."

You see, old Raymond Crowder was a Saturday morning regular here at Cut N Shoot and knew the value of a good drive down the throat.

★ ★ ★

It wasn't hard for me to find Thumper. I just plain followed his ass from the church tent to the clubhouse.

"Nice turnout, wasn't it?" He stopped on the cedar porch and took his usual position against the railing.

"Uh, huh." Although it hadn't been one of those more posing questions, I went ahead and replied. I also went no further than that less-than-learned response. I was going to see just how long it took him to bring up the greens and what he'd done, or rather not done, to them.

We both stood there waiting for the other to interrupt our silence. He broke first, but like an open-faced putt, he broke right of the cup. "How about a beer?"

"Nope." I finally realized that if I had to wait on him, I would miss my tee time, still two hours off. Since he had obviously given me the honors, I hit first. "What's the deal, Thump? We ain't got no left-handers anywhere near the top out there today." It was not one of your more point-blank queries, and yet it was.

"I just decided to let you boys play a regular game of golf. No tricks. All you gotta do is go out and play the course as it lies."

95

"That ain't near good enough and you know it." I was not accepting his reasoning. He was hiding something and there was a better than par chance that he wasn't going to tell me what it was.

"That's all, slick. Just a right fair game of golf." I'd learned over the years that once he called me by that name, he had made his point and there was little I could do to change the outcome. To prove his point, he turned and headed inside.

I caught him with the screen half open for one final question. This one was just to show there were no hard feelings. "Denise didn't leave any surprises you would care to tell me about?"

"Not this time. We played indoors." He completed his journey into his lair, his secret still intact.

It would be a while before he owned up to the sad fact that he had shot his wad on the pin placements the previous three rounds. He had just plain run out of tricks. He had used up all the treacherous locations and he couldn't go back and use them again. It just wouldn't be golf.

I strolled over to Number 1 and watched some of the higher scores begin their rounds. They attacked this now fairly easy hole with such reckless abandon that birdies fell mortally wounded, left and right. As I watched, one eagle was even pulled from its perch and slaughtered. The first one of the tournament.

While I was planning my hoped-for strategy on this beginning hole, old Number 99 happened

upon the scene and asked me what I thought of
last night's sports telecast. I had completely
forgotten about my little interview after
yesterday's round and that it was going to be
on the late evening news. Since I wasn't about
to lie to this gentle giant, I told him the TV
in Patsy's office had been out, so I missed my
debut. Now it wasn't your outright lie cause
Patsy had used both plugs in her office to hook
up her stereo system for the rink music, which
meant she had to unhook the TV to accomplish
that feat. I begged his forgiveness and asked
if he could possibly make me a tape of the
broadcast for posterity's sake. He said he
could and that he was sorry I missed it. I told
him **I** surely was.

I noticed his companion for the tournament
wasn't at his side, so I changed the almost
touchy subject and asked where old Brucie was
hiding out. He went on to tell me that Brucie
was helping the fellow with the mini-cam get
things set up for some last-minute interviews
before they made their way up the tower. His
short reaction to my question led me to believe
that he was probably glad to be rid of his
sidekick for the time being. I started to ask
him if he was enjoying his pairing for the
tournament, but I decided not to press my luck.

Out of the corner of my eye, I saw that Brucie
had finished his preparation and was heading
this way, mini-cammed helper and all. I quickly
excused myself from the big guy, explaining
that I had some last-minute things to attend
to, and that he, being a fairly good golfer
himself, could understand that. He said he sure
did and wished me good luck as I headed off in
a direction opposite of Brucie's oncoming path.

I had been about everywhere I needed to go, but still had more than an hour before it was my time to play. I needed to find something to keep my mind full, otherwise old Father Psyche would probably try and lay a little bit of reverse psychology on my feeble brain.

I thought about seeing if my caddie needed any last-minute help cleaning my clubs or anything else caddies do before a big match like this, but I had used Carey several times before and understood that my tools were probably already cleaned and polished and sitting by my locker like a loaded gun.

Melanie, whom I hadn't seen since early this morning, was already at her leader board station, although she would have nothing to write down for a few hours. Right now, she was mainly there for show, and a fine choice, I might add.

I saw movement over on the practice range, unfamiliar but familiar enough to revive my memory. I decided a small scotch was in order for the moment, as waiting was not one of my strong suits. On the way over to the tent, which was serving a multitude of purposes today, I ran across Denise, all decked out in her finest revealing halter-top. I stopped long enough to ask her how she was enjoying her visit to our establishment, a loaded question to say the least. All she could muster up in that pretty little empty head of hers was "Fine". I decided to continue on with my journey as she obviously had no idea who I was or why I would ask her such a silly question.

At the bar, I asked for and received a dual-purpose Styrofoam cup, half filled with scotch poured lightly over ice. It made for a refreshing lunch after my late breakfast.

B.J. arrived in time to settle my fraying nerves with light conversation. He reminded me that I had better keep my eyes open in front of me cause he was only two back and he had every intention of burning up my daddy's course today. He said he'd done bought two airline tickets back to Arizona. One for him and one for that big old trophy that was sitting up on the stage that the preacher had long since vacated. I told him to give it his best shot, but not to look back cause I would sure as hell be there grinning.

Spook Taylor joined us for some last-minute, needless chit-chat, so we rehashed our intentions, solely for his young benefit.

The announcer by Number 1 had just announced the twosome ahead of them, so we all wished each other false good luck as they left.

I was down to my last half hour and the butterflies in my stomach knew it. I decided a trip to the john was called for, and with any luck, I would be able to pass the last few minutes in deep, comfortable concentration.

I knew enough not to check to see if my playing partner had arrived on the scene yet. He wasn't about to break from his usual routine for my benefit. So, I made my way to the locker room for a final sit and think.

I accomplished a little more than to relieve myself of my morning coffee, but remained seated until I heard my name called to the Number 1 tee.

As I exited, I saw Kelly Dale crossing Whipoorwill. I knew he would make one stop at the tent before joining me, so I stepped back in and watched him through the partially opened door.

Psyche time would start now. I let him arrive at the tee box first, a feeling unknown to him, then I made my way to our meeting amidst the throng of applause, less than deafening, but still there.

It was for me they were applauding and he knew it.

★★★

This was the first time I had met the kid face-to-face. He wasn't anything more than your All-American Boy. Natural straight blonde hair, slightly bleached by hours in the sun and cut evenly, just over the ears. I judged him to be about five ten in Footjoys and not an ounce of fat showing on his still young frame. By all rights, his eyes should have been blue, but they sparkled emerald against the course. With the exception of his eyes and an inch or two, he could have been me at that age. But my years had added pounds and my vanity, longer hair and a mustache. We were no longer the same.

We stood there staring at each other, like two boxers ready for the bell, then he grinned. "Nice move."

I returned his smile, shrugging my shoulders and raising my palms skyward as an acknowledging gesture. My ploy had worked. I held out my hand and he took it. "Good luck, son."

The thought had crossed my mind earlier to throw the same line at him as Bubba had done to me when first we played, but now I was glad I hadn't. I held no animosity for this man, either as a golfer or as a person. We were both here for the sport, and no matter what game was being played in our minds, consciously or subconsciously, it was still golf that had brought us together. And golf we would play.

As the announcer told the audience that we were the last group of the day, I offered him the honors. He accepted and stepped between the championship markers. He waited until the man with the microphone explained to the crowd that we were tied for the lead, not that they didn't know that already, before sending his Pinnacle no less than three hundred and ten yards straight up the tree-lined fairway and onto the front of the green.

It was now my turn to wait as the gallery applauded his effort. As we exchanged places, I casually questioned him about whether that was as far as he could hit the ball. He answered quickly, advising me that he wanted to leave me something to get inside of.

And that I did. My drive had not been nearly as straight and perfect as his, but I got your usual country club bounce from the right side of the fairway, allowing my Top Flight to skirt the leading edge of the bunker and onto the green. He had a more even putt, but I was closer by two feet.

The first hole shrank up to about the size of a dime as his first shot on the green dropped in for an eagle. I don't know why I even thought he would miss. I had seen him at work yesterday.

I knew from experience that my putt would break a hair left, so I played it accordingly and matched his score. Two under with seventeen left to play. Not a bad start, but I was dreaming if I thought I could keep that up. I just hoped he couldn't.

Kelly walked along the edge of Crystal Creek ahead of me to Number 2, the hardest damned hole on the course. The five hundred and ninety-nine yards wasn't too awful for a par 5, but the fact that it horseshoed around a cliff that couldn't be cut would have made it a par 7, if such a number existed in the golf annals.

Kelly hit a heavy fade that brought him around the first bend and again into the center of the fairway. He wouldn't be on in two, but three would be easy.

I took a different route and played long up the left side and almost over-stroked the ball, stopping just short of the sand at the back of the first dog-leg. My position left me out for the next shot.

Conversation would not be possible as we traversed opposite sides of the fairway. Since I had stopped no more than a foot in front of the bunker, I left myself with no other alternative but to assume a stance in the sand for my next shot. The ball would fly from that position with a natural slice, meaning I had to compensate for it; otherwise, I would careen off the canyon wall to God knows where. Overcompensation would land me in the sand on the opposite side. Carey was holding my three wood, which I exchanged for a five and lifted the ball up and around the wall to the middle

of the approach fairway, one hundred and twenty
yards out. I could see a birdie in the making,
but wasn't yet about to count its eggs.

Kelly took a five iron and laid a perfect
fade around the bend about forth yards behind
me. It was still his turn. We had a slight
breeze in our faces, which is probably why he
took one too much stick on his next shot and
landed it on the back of the green. Still, he
was on in three.

I studied his shot, as good golfers do, and
figured the wind not to be much of a factor. I
quickly realized the error of my decision as I
left a wedge shot way short of the pin on the
front. The eggs were slipping away.

We both managed routine pars and accepted our
fate.

I decided to break the silence again as we
stepped out onto the peninsula that acted as
the Number 3 tee box. "I don't suppose you've
found the water here yet, have you?"

"Not yet, but there's always that chance."
He let my question slide off his back like
water off a duck.

He didn't find it this time either, laying a
three iron six feet from the flag on the island
green. I followed suit and considered myself
fortunate as my line drive barely cleared the
railroad ties that elevated the green in the
middle of the lake and rolled across it to the
back and almost in on the other side. I prayed
to get down in two.

Young Mr. Dale sank his birdie putt after I
managed to get close enough on my second shot
for a tap-in. Although I thanked the golf god

for allowing me to save par, I was now one down. But there were still plenty of holes to be screwed up.

Number 4 was the course's answer to a cluster-fuck. An offshoot of Crystal Creek snakes, no less than eight times across the four hundred and twenty-five yard fairway, before completely circling the green. The edges of the fairway are lined with sand traps and pampas grass, both of which will make an easy meal of a golfer's ball, should the water refuse to drink. The requirement on this par 4 is nothing more than blind luck.

Kelly still had the honors and drove blindly and drowned his in the fifth bend in the snake. I found the luck, barely clearing the fourth bend and bouncing to a stop way short of where Kelly had entered the creek on the fly. After it was all said and done and the penalties applied, I managed an easy par and Kelly took a bogey.

After four holes, we were back to where we had started, only better off. We weren't beating each other, but we were beating the course.

My playing partner walked off the green like he had just birdied the hole. I thought about mentioning the fact that we had just traded holes or that it had taken me four holes to wrestle the honors away from him, but I remembered what had happened the last time I tried my hand at polite conversation. It was me who screwed up and ended up down.

He waited to the side of the tee box for me to step up and hit. Out of all the holes, Number 5 is probably my favorite, long and lovely.

Along both sides of the seven hundred and one-yard fairway stand rows and rows of nothing but rows and rows of tall pines. Walking down this pine tunnel, you can hear a whisper echo and today's slight breeze was breaking through the needles like the sound of waves washing ashore. If God ever did vacation from Heaven, He did it right here.

I blasted the sweetest drive I had managed in ages, splitting this old fairway in half with a three hundred and fifty yarder, give or take a foot or two. I also managed to keep it to the left in order to work a draw to pay dirt. I shot a daring glance at Kelly, threatening him to better that one.

Without a word or even a return, a silent answer, he stepped into place and let it all out. He was answering me with strength; his first mistake. It would have been a close contest, had not that last pine jumped out in front of his downward arc, sending his shot deep into the woods. This was **definitely** my favorite hole.

Kelly would shoot two more times before I would hit again, but at least he regained his composure and played like a true golfer. He had a slight opening in the direction of the green, but not much. Rather than take the duffer's choice, he played back left and safely to the fairway. From there, he crunched a long and lean two wood within two hundred yards of the pin.

I responded once again to the challenge and flat hit my three-wood dead into the throat, coming up short of my driving distance by a mere fifty yards, leaving me about that same amount of stretching fairway to the green. Kelly ironed his way onto the green, but got maximum roll and ended just off the back between the bushes. I started to ask the golf god why he hadn't allowed him to roll up under one of them things instead of betwixt 'em, but from my position on this hole, that would have been like asking for rain in the midst of a flood.

Kelly managed to get up and down in two for your natural bogey, while I chipped close enough and one-putted for your one better than natural bogey. God, how I loved this hole!

I was now one up and still under par, with visions of breaking the course record, not to mention winning this here tournament. I should have reminded myself of what Daddy used to tell me when things looked bad, cause it also fit when things were kind of rosy.

"Hang in there, son. It'll eventually get worse."

And that it did. Number 6 is your basic, unparable par 3. The yardage reads two forty-seven, but the second half is solid water all the way to the green. Your smarter golfer will accept what he sees and just lay up and hope to put his second shot near the pin and scramble for par. While your heavy-handed linkster, like myself today, will hang it all out to dry in an attempt to drive the water and stay on the horizontally narrow green. What usually happens to folks like myself is we either hit it extremely fat and deep six the ball or we burn the green and end up in the back bunker, or worse, under the pampas grass.

I managed the latter. Thumper always told me I wasn't way up there on the smart leader board. I never did find my Top Flight in that grassy bush and had to settle for a gut-wrenching double bogey.

Kelly took advantage of playing behind me and lay up, but shanked his second shot to the far right of the green and carded an honest bogey. We were head up again, but now only one under.

I had been what Daddy called the author of my own misfortune.

Number 7 is your basic three hundred- and ninety-six-yard dog-leg left, with water beginning just before the leg on the right and running all the way to the green. If the golfer can hit his drive all two hundred yards in the air while maintaining an elevation of one hundred and fifty feet above sea level, he can clear the tall pines to the left. However, the money ain't in it.

We both hit your basic straight drives past the cut, like you're supposed to, and arrived on the green in two. However, it took us the same number of strokes to put our little balls in the cup. The pars would still keep us under for the round this far.

Number 8, believe it or not, is only the second hardest hole on the course. I would argue that handicap with almost anyone, but the scorecard never changed. It's so mean that words cannot explain it, but I'll try.

To start out, it is six hundred and fifty yards long, but not as the crow flies. The narrow fairway begins straight but then turns a dog-leg to the right. There are short pines, right at seventy-five feet high, to the right of the cut. They can be flown; however, where the trees stop, water starts on the same side. If you don't fly true, you're wet. On the same cut, but to the back of the fairway, is a lake. The lake will not come into play until your second shot. About a hundred and eighty yards past the first dog-leg is the second, only this one shoots left. About two hundred yards down the last fairway is the green, only it also sits directly off the left and behind the more adult pines, which cannot be flown, unless by helicopter. The green cannot be reached in two. Never has, never will. If the golfer can fly the first set of trees at the cut and manage to stay dry, he might be able to get on in three. However, what happens most of the time is they get the big head after clearing the first trees and feel all powerful enough to do the same by the green and always end up in the lake that extends from the back of the first cut to the tall pines that protect the green. I guess I don't need to tell you it is a par 5.

If you are thoroughly confused by the description, try playing the mother fucker!

Kelly played the hole like a natural, straight up the fairway to the first dog-leg, then through the second. He put his third shot up the last straightaway, pin high but not yet on the putting surface. He did, however, chip close enough to one-putt. You take your par, be happy with it and go on to the next hole.

But not old Joe Don! Hell no! The only thing I learned back on Number 6 was nothing. I drove the first cut and into the lateral water. I tried to make up for being stupid by playing even more stupid. I knew I couldn't make the green but I tried to power it in anyway. I duck-hooked that sucker, all right hand, mind you, into the lateral lake on the left. My last drop did allow me to chip onto the green, where I matched Kelly in putts but not in score. I was one down again.

All my sweet ass had to do after my first screw-up was to keep it right and I could have salvaged a par with some luck. Carey refused to let me have my towel cause he was dearly afraid I would tie it to a local pine tree and attempt to hang myself; not that it would have been any loss. I guess he was just trying to protect his tip.

Number 9 needs no further description and by that time, the cameras were rolling, as was my head. After what I had seen Kelly accomplish on this hole the day before, I knew I had my work cut out for me. If I could just match him breast for breast, I would be happy to go into the back nine one down.

As it was, I managed to play better for the local TV viewers. Kelly arrived on the green, but just on the front. He under-swung, if such a shot is possible on this hole, and came up short, barely missing the rocky wall as it fell. I, in turn, gently slapped mine to within inches of where he had rested the day before and gratefully acknowledged and accepted the birdie putt. Kelly took par.

I touched my cap in appreciation of the gallery's applause, if not for my own dumb luck, as Kelly hurriedly left the green for the tent. I hoped he had a mind to try some of Lamar's southern fried chicken legs.

In my own haste to grab a nerve-killing scotch before continuing, I failed to inspect the leader board. I guess my mind felt safe to be even with my co-leader and one under at that juncture.

★★★

My watch told me it was three-fifteen, which meant we had finished the front in the regulation two hours. If we could manage the same on the back, it would leave us with fifteen minutes of airtime. Plenty of time for the presentation of the winner to be viewed live and in color. If we took any longer, we would just be shit out of luck as the Astros game began at five-thirty and for some odd reason, they carried more weight than us on Channel 3.

I looked around for Kelly, but he was nowhere in sight. Figuring he had already returned to the course, I downed my scotch and hit the road. I passed Chris Carmichael on my way over and from the hurt puppy look in his eyes, I could see that he obviously had not shot well enough for an automatic invitation back. I chose to remain silent as he ambled by.

I then remembered the leaderboard but decided not to go back, as time was of the essence if we were to hold court on live TV at the end.

Sure enough, Kelly Dale was there waiting. It wouldn't have been polite to go ahead and tee off. No, because I wasn't there yet, but because big old me had won the honors.

"Feel up to nine more?" I asked, half-jokingly.

"If that's what it takes," he answered and stepped back off the box to let me begin.

I pasted what I thought was a fairly good drive down the middle of the fairway, but when it reached its apex about two hundred down, it sort of hung there in the breeze and died. I saw the huge cross bunker below it, but still figured I had gotten enough into it to clear, but I was sadly mistaken. The ball landed in the back of the sand trap that divides the fairway into two. A two-hundred-and-forty-yard sand shot on a par 4 is not totally out of the question, unless, of course, you have to negotiate a creek the last twenty yards.

Kelly kept his shot quail high and flew the trap with no problem, putting himself in what is commonly known in golf circles as Position A.

Since I had a fried egg lie, I decided to finally play it safe. I executed a high looper out of the man-made desert and found the center of the fairway a good twenty yards from the water.

Kelly tried to make the game interesting by landing on the green before rolling into the left bunker, which, all in all, was not that bad a position. He could pick it out and near the pin. Lord knows he practiced that shot just yesterday and succeeded.

Water has always given me problems. Just knowing it is lurking there in front of me is enough to make me choke. I didn't quite choke this time, but I did over-stick, which on the pro tour means the same thing. I came to rest on the back of the green and a country mile from the pin.

As described, Kelly picked his Pinnacle out of the sand and damn near holed it, sliding within a hair of the cup on the left. He went ahead and tapped in his par to give me a clear shot to tie.

I didn't. As a matter of fact, I didn't even get there. I left myself a six-foot knee-knocker and downhill to boot. I hoped that mid-game scotch had been enough to calm my yips. My trusty putting iron seemed to weigh a ton as I brought it hopefully straight back. I hit the cup dead on the back lip and held my breath as it bounced back against the front and finally plopped in the hole. It was a bogey, but I counted myself lucky, considering the alternative.

I found myself one down to my closest competitor again, but I had been there before. I could tell Kelly was breathing somewhat easier, thanks to me, and I let him know it. "Reckon I ought to just concede now and save us both the trouble?"

"It's not over yet, sir."

"Sir? What was this sir shit?" I thought to myself. I tried hard but couldn't muster up a suitable reply.

Number 11 mirrors Number 10, only back, slightly uphill in the opposite direction. The sand halfway there would not come into play as the slight wind was now at our backs.

Kelly rifled his same down-the-pike drive and I followed, yard for yard. We came up looking like snake eyes on the second tier. As my lie was to the left, I hit first and again found the back of the green, thanks mostly to the wind. Kelly went to school on my shot with one less iron to the front, where we both two-putted for pars. By all rights, he should have gone two up on me, as his first putt rimmed the cup but failed to fall in the back door.

From the tee box, Number 12 looks relatively easy. It plays one hundred and fifty yards to the green, elevated a good one hundred feet above the tee. What the first-time golfer cannot see with the naked eye is the sand moat that completely surrounds the putting surface. The object here is just to get to the hundred-foot level, whether you make the sand or the green. Anything else has a better than average chance of rolling down the grassy hill on any side.

We both played to the sky and into the mouth of the mesa. We wouldn't know until we got there how well we fared. As it was, we both found sand, only this time we had switched places, with me in the front and he in the back. I jokingly told Carey there was a pair of extra golf gloves in my bag he could use if he started getting rake blisters, after I managed to lay my second shot four feet short.

Kelly was a little closer on his side, but not by much. I sank mine then prayed for the miracle which was not to come. He stepped up and sank his without so much as a practice swing. I understood now whose side the old golf god was on today and it sure wasn't mine.

Number 13 is pretty, but it will eat your sack lunch. If you've ever flown to California by way of Arizona, then this hole won't take much explanation. The tee box is an extension of the Number 12 green and the hole is no more than fifty to eighty yards away, depending on Thumper's mood the night before. Today it plays at sixty-five. The green is at the same altitude as the tee box, but as you will recall, that's your basic hundred feet above everyone and everything else. Between the two plateaus meanders another offshoot of Crystal Creek. If you find yourself in the rocky terrain that leads downhill to the creek and up the other slope to the green, you might as well just write that ball off and hit again. If you intend on missing the green, you'd best do it on one of the other three sides. At least there you may have a shot. No promises, you understand.

Kelly grabbed a thumb and forefinger pinch of grass and tested the crosswind. In our previous rounds, we had both managed two pars and a bogey on this hole, so we knew where it was and how to get there. But history would not repeat itself here today. My young partner hit a fat wedge onto the far rocks and then looked to the heavens. I secretly apologized to the golf god for doubting his presence at my side and stepped up for my turn at bat. The golf god must be of Mexican descent, because he flat made me chili-dip mine into the creek below. Had we been in non-tournament play, we would have probably allowed each other a mulligan and started over. But we couldn't.

We tried a little harder this time and arrived at our intended destination, but just barely, and we were already lying par and nowhere near paydirt. If you non-players don't think a shitty shot will put a death-grip on your family jewels, then you didn't watch us putt. We didn't come within a foot of the cup as we rolled past and had to settle for a couple of ten-footers just to save buzzard, which we did.

We were both now on the plus side of par for the first time today and I was still coming up the rear. I finally realized that this thing was about to draw to a close. If I didn't make my move and soon, then I was going to be one hell of a disappointment to myself, not to mention Mama. And shit! Don't forget Thumper. I would have to live with him for a good year before I got another chance to redeem myself. The thought even hit me that my redemption might never come, since Kelly would probably turn pro after this.

Kelly still had the honors at Number 14, which lays out to be a four hundred- and seventy-five-yard par 4, ninety-degree dog-leg right. It would be simple enough if Daddy hadn't left that two-hundred-year-old oak tree right smack dab in the middle of the fairway at the cut. Not to mention the fairway is lined with unflyable pines. I won't even mention the two other pines that stand in front corners of the green like goal posts without a crossbar.

With a one-stroke lead, on me at least, he decided to play safe and drive straight up the middle, short of the oak. Carey had seen me play this hole and reminded me of what I needed to do, not that I needed his cue, but I thanked him anyway. I played my power fade, which still remains my best shot, and damn near caught one of the pines on the left as it left the tee box. I was on my tiptoes as I watched that little white globe sail from left to right and finally bounce to the right of that old oak and head for the center of the approach fairway. Although it rolled out of sight, I was fairly certain I was in perfect line for your natural three points through the piney uprights.

Kelly's ball had landed a little too close to the oak tree, meaning he had to keep his next shot low to avoid the spreading branches above. He came out sizzling but amputated a limb from the right pine at the gateway and dropped short.

I made my field goal, dead center, and nestled up close to the flag. Kelly got up and down in two but it wasn't good enough, as my one-putt put me back in the hunt.

Next came your basic, stupid dog-leg par 3. Daddy never studied golf courses much before building this one or he would have known you don't do that to holes that you're supposed to reach from the tee box. Course, he would have probably done it anyway, considering the mood he was obviously in at the time.

Although I had finally won the honors again, I had never been able to move my power fade down from my woods to my irons. I thought about going with my five wood and went so far as to ask Carey for it, but the little sucker refused to relinquish it. I realized then what I was paying him for, cause too much bending would put me dead into the woods with no hope of staying alive. Instead, he handed me a four iron, which I graciously accepted without further hesitation. At two hundred and fifteen yards, I could punch that club up handy, and I did just that.

Kelly followed my lead and once again we snake-eyed, only this time he was left and I got to play schoolboy. He pitched up close, but I got closer. Not that it made any difference, as we both one-putted.

It was looking more and more like the golf god didn't favor either of us today. He obviously didn't have a bet down.

The next hole and the one after would be the test. Number 16 tees off in the shallow Crystal Creek valley. The tight twenty-yard-wide fairway starts uphill for one hundred and fifty yards before leveling off for fifty yards. This is followed by a one-hundred-yard rise to another fifty-yard plane. Finally, and if your heart can take it, you get to hit another shot of some two hundred and fifty yards uphill to the green. Your third fifty-yard plane. If you only get to the front of the green, you will find yourself putting forever. No matter how you count it, that is six hundred long-ass yards. To the pin today it plays six hundred and twenty-five. Since trees refuse to grow on this part of the course, the rough is strictly as Webster defined it:

> "Having an uneven surface; course;
> turbulent; agitated; violent; rude;
> etc."

The same rocks that were plentiful at Number 13 had multiplied like little bunnies and immigrated to these parts. There was a little green matter growing throughout, after all, this is a golf course and cactus does, at times, look like rocks. Many a misplaced shot has ended up in sole possession of the rough's natural inhabitant. A golf ball does bear a striking resemblance to a timber rattler's egg. The course rules do allow the player a free drop from that lie, even in tournament play, as that is one loose impediment no golfer would dare try to remove.

For the smart, safe golfer, the object is to just hit from plane to plane and make damn sure you stay on the playing surface. If you can muster that little feat, you will find yourself gratefully on the putting surface. By that time, you won't give a nasty shit how close you are to the flag.

This is also one of the few par fives where you don't hit a wood until your third shot. However, since most of your everyday golfers ain't all that smart, the vast majority of them will try to power the ball to the second plane and will either land on the second hill, if they're lucky, or end up in a match play contest with Mr. Rattler. Either way, they're dead meat cause there ain't a duffer alive that can hit straight from an uphill lie.

Kelly and I, with me as the lead-off man, played true to the cause and laid up on the first level spot in the fairway. Knowing we didn't have a four-hundred-plus shot in our bags, we did the same on the second. From there, our status as better-than-average thinking golfers buried its blonde head in a snake hole. We both knew what other golfers know. The closer you get to the pin on your third shot, the better your chances of a birdie. We both yanked out two woods, the most god-awfulest club in anyone's bag, for the last two hundred and fifty some-odd yards. The rest is history. He went left and I went right and neither of us reached our objective. Hell, we didn't even manage to stay on the close-cut green stuff. We did, however, manage to remain unfanged and reached the final plateau in four. From there, we scrambled in two-putts and settled for bogeys.

We were now plus two for the round, with the same number to play. I had ended with that fair number before and had every intention of doing it again. I finally accepted the fact that no record would fall my way today, but I could win this here thing by at least tying my own.

We walked straight over to Number 17, a short walk since the tee box starts directly at the back of sixteen's green. Daddy must have figured that all clean-living golfers deserved a second chance at going to hell, cause this hole took up where the last one left off. It was the same shit all over again, only this time the two-hundred-and-fifty-yard hill exchanged places with the one hundred and fifty-yarder. You could now get your wood shot out of the way first, if not forever. The only major problem was that you were so dog-tired after negotiating sixteen's mountain, you may not have a two hundred and fifty yarder left in you.

I proved the point, or rather my middle age did, and only managed a little over two hundred yards. It didn't really scare me to death since I could hit from an uphill lie. I had read all the books. What did throw a little fright into me was my playing partner. He definitely showed his young age to the gallery-ites by slobber-knocking his drive clean to the flat grass. A smile erupted on his cherub-like face for the first time in several holes, as he turned and almost double-timed his way up the center of the fairway. It was his way of showing me that it definitely was **not** over yet.

I four-ironed my way to the middle of the second shelf and breathed a sigh of relief, knowing he would also have to join me or die.

My breathing came even easier when I topped the first rise and caught a glimpse of his lie. He had actually pounded his drive three hundred yards to the inch, acceptable on a straight, level fairway, but certainly not here. His Pinnacle was resting right smack dab where the back of the tier begins its ascent. It was almost as bad as being up against a grassy wall. He would have to take nothing more than a wedge to obtain relief. We would most definitely be no worse than together when we hit.

He took his club back like a pro, but caught too much of the big ball first and barely made it halfway up the second hill. His age was now starting to show in reverse order as he stormed up to his lie and hit it again without even so much as a practice swing this time. He flew the pad and landed on the uphill slope, and I truly accepted my one-shot advantage for the moment. I thought about making some kind of crude remark, but figured it would be needless as he was now his own worst enemy.

With my advantage in mind, I decided not to go head-on for the pin. If I could just make the green and two putts, I would probably go into the final hole one fine stroke up. Not a terribly bad place to be.

I carried out my plan and landed fifteen yards onto the front of the green, thirty feet from the cup. Still in semi-disarray, Kelly did manage to make the putting surface, but outside of me. I marked my ball and watched.

I caught several deep breaths as they entered his lungs before he positioned himself on the correct side of his ball and slapped a putt into gimme range. I nodded my approval for him to putt out and he did with little or no problem or practice.

I eased back behind my ball to check the breaks and found none. "Thank you, Thumper," I mumbled to myself. All I needed to do was get close. A bird would nail the lid shut, but all I wanted to do now was close it. I felt a bead of sweat trickle down the middle of my back as I bent over to putt. As soon as my blade made contact, I knew the viewers back home were gasping. I had opened my club face in my extended take-back and left it there. I squeezed my eyes shut because there was no reason to watch. I knew where it would end up. I opened them slowly, only to find out that I had been correct. My ball had rolled wide right, leaving me with no less than ten feet of earth to travel.

I scared myself into coming up short on my next putt and backhanded the last one into the cup. The final hole would decide the winner, just as it should.

I still had a shot at tying my own record for a third time, but so did Kelly. My tired brain was suddenly impregnated by the horrible realization that we couldn't end in a tie. Our tournament rules forbade. It was one of our unwritten rules. There had to be an out-and-out winner. In the case of ties for the ten returning players, we had always gone back to the scorecard; however, there had never been a tie for the number one spot. Someone had always managed to outdo the rest. If Kelly and I ended this hole the same way we started, we would be forced into a playoff. Nothing less than your basic Sudden Death.

Thumper and I had decided not to follow the pros' guidelines and start no further than the fifteenth hole. We had agreed that if we were ever faced with such a dilemma, we would go all the way back to the beginning. We figured it would be quicker as someone would surely find a birdie on the first hole and end the suffering. And that is exactly what I was doing now; suffering. If we had to keep on the course past the regulation amount of holes, I would surely come out on the losing end. Kelly had proved that with his drive. There was no doubt in my feeble mind that he still had enough strong, young blood pumping through his veins to lay a driver clean out of sight, or at least the three hundred and five yards needed to put him on the putting surface if need be.

I hadn't realized it but I had been standing on the tee box staring off into space. I was brought back to realization when my empty eyes focused on the whirring mini-cam that had just taken a position to the right of the tee box.

Ahead of me now was the enemy. The Chute! When Daddy had completed seventeen holes, he must have realized that he had to get golfers back down the mountain he had placed them on after the last two holes. By that time, he was obviously ready to give them a break, while at the same time not giving them something entirely ordinary to shoot at. One ordinary hole on the course, Number 1, was enough. So, he took the natural hill and placed bunkers along both sides. He then bladed a thirty-five-yard wide, shallow trench between them and created a nine-hundred-yard chute to the green. It wasn't your basic long par 5. It was a half mile, transcending the definition of long. But it was all downhill. If a player could maintain a suitable amount of height on his drive while keeping it dead center, he could go home and brag to his companions about the five-hundred-yard drive he had mastered at the Cut N Shoot Golf Club.

However, any first bounce more than five yards to the left or right of center would carry the shot centrifugally into one of the bunkers. From that point, he would never find the center of the green path again. Daddy giveth, yet Daddy taketh away.

It didn't take much deliberation for me to decide upon my club selection. Carey had already unsheathed my three wood and was pointing it at me like a saber. The boy could read me like an open book. I didn't have the yardage with this club, but for height and accuracy, it was the best my bag had to offer. I took an easy swing and prayed as the golf god returned to my side in enough time to carry my ball high and dead center, and then let it return to earth to rest four hundred yards down the home stretch. That little white dot never even thought of straying.

Kelly chose his driver for his weapon. It too had been an easy choice for him, as he had already proven, to me at least, that he had full command of that club. I found this time to be no different as he slammed a late riser through the low afternoon air, finally halting a good fifty yards ahead of me. We would be going down to the wire together, and then some.

We were left with no choice but to walk together down what I hoped would be the final fairway. It crossed my mind, though only momentarily, to ask him how his old daddy was doing, but I figured he had to already know that I was on to him. Still, we had come this far together and chances were we would be continuing, so a little conversation might break whatever spell was controlling his game.

"Why ain't you turned professional yet, son? If you hadn't shown up here this week, I would be having me a nice, leisurely, afternoon stroll down this here fairway right about now."

"I think you know why, sir." There he went with that sir shit again. "And I didn't just show up. You invited me, remember?"

He answered my questions to the letter. Even the one I had chosen not to ask. I was glad to see that I had reached my drive cause I was done with inquiries. The conversation had been short but damn sure to the point.

I had not bothered to give my three wood back to Carey, cause I purely intended to dance with it again. And that I did. I added another three hundred and forty yards to my count and now stood ready for no more than a nine iron and then home.

Kelly blasted me again, although he did have a fifty-yard head start. He lost twenty yards to stroke, but was still thirty steps in front of me. I knew I had to get close enough for no more than one strike with my putter, and that would probably be just good enough to finish the round locked in a tie.

I have no idea how high I placed my approach shot since the rough was bare of the usual pines, but I thought that mother was going to hang up there forever. If that happened, I would have to declare a lost ball and wind up losing this thing. When it did finally land, it took one bounce, backed up and died, six long but beautiful feet from the flag. I laid a loving kiss on that club before giving it back to Carey and telling him to be gentle with her, cause she'd done given herself to me willingly and I would damn sure respect her in the morning.

I finally outdid Kelly so far on this hole, as he left a wedge on the front and a good twenty feet away.

I knew this tournament of ours wasn't being beamed by satellite back to Connecticut, but I made a right proud mental note to make sure a videotape was. I had probably sunk a couple thousand six-footers over the years and even probably missed a few hundred, but right now I wasn't thinking about those hundred as I marked my ball so Kelly could finish.

A foggy hush fell on the gallery as Kelly putted, then lifted almost as quickly when the ball fell in. I did nothing more than stand there and quiver my putter right out of my grip, as he bent down to retrieve his ball from the shallow well. He did so on instinct, as his eyes were staring clean through mine.

As the crowd's roar was dying down, I went through the silent motions of replacing my ball and then bent down behind it as if to offer my final prayer to the golf god. Those missed hundreds now filled my head as they drove the thousands off the field of battle. I must have putted with my eyes closed, as I swear I never saw the putt drop in.

But it did!

All I could think of was how desperately I needed a scotch. I was completely drained, both physically and emotionally. I needed something stronger than Pepsi if I was going to match the drive Kelly would unmercifully throw at me when we started again. I realized I had forgotten to take my ball out of the cup, but when I turned to go back, I saw the flag waving at me in the breeze. Carey must have come to my rescue again.

As I left the green and headed for the tent, I remembered our TV schedule and checked my watch. It was five-fifteen. We had at least kept to our timetable, but all for naught. We would easily chew up the last quarter hour on the first hole of our playoff, leaving no time to preview the winner. As long as it was me accepting that big old trophy, then I figured it wouldn't matter too awful much.

I looked up to the tower but it was empty. An idea occurred to me that maybe Billy Ray and Brucie had decided to man the mini-cam out on the course. That way, they might be able to hold the presentation right there on Number 1 green, should we bring this match to a conclusion right then and there.

Something appeared to be wrong with the flow of the crowd. From what just happened with me and Kelly on eighteen, the gallery should be hastily making their way to Number 1. Instead, they were filing past me toward the tent. I also noticed that Carey and my bag were heading for the lockers. I started after him, but my journey was halted in mid-stride by Thumper's voice as it amplified about the immediate area.

The crowd, another record attendance this year, was too thick to wade through, so I made my way right. I saw Melanie at the leaderboard, but the name at the top wasn't mine, not Kelly's. I stopped, open-mouthed, and read the top line.

TAYLOR, S   4 5 3 4 5 3 4 5 3 4 4 3 3 4 3 5 5 5 72-78-75-225

Spook Taylor had done gone out there today and shot level par. He now owned the course record, not to mention this here tournament. The boy had obviously played the course, unlike the two names that fell below his.

At least Melanie had seen fit to place my name next in line above Kelly's, although we shared the same number. I would have to thank her later, in my own way, of course.

I took my defeat like the man I hoped I was and joined Spook and Thumper on the stage in just enough time to help my buddy lift that huge, gold-plated monstrosity into Spook's waiting arms.

I was questionably amazed at how good I felt at that moment, even though I had just given away what I had hoped would be mine. There wasn't room for two of them things in my trophy case anyway and they were too big for bookends.

As Spook was making his acceptance speech, I surveyed the crowd about the tent. I saw the young man who was no longer my arch-rival standing near the bar, beer in hand. As our eyes met, he winked and I knew it was truly over. I could accept the fact that I hadn't beaten him at this game, cause he hadn't beaten me either. The status quo still remained, and

there was no way he would be back. With any
luck at all, since he had the skill part locked
up, he would be on the pro tour before the
summer events got hot and heavy.

I left the stage so this year's winner could
bask in all the TV glory alone. Billy Ray wasted
no time in getting Spook to comment to his
viewing audience his future plans. As I was
walking away, I heard the names of several of
your big-time professional tournaments being
laid out, so my mind crossed out another name
for next year's list of invitees. I guess Spook
had figured out a way to beat his fear of
flying, just as he had figured out how to beat
this here golf course.

When I finally reached the bar, Kelly was
gone. I grabbed me a tall scotch anyway, and
for the first time since early this morning, I
just let my worn-out mind rest.

I traded casual conversation with those
gathered around me, golfers and non-golfers
alike, until the afternoon sun reached down and
clung to the top of the pines. The crowd was
thinning as they made their way to their
respective means of transportation. Most of the
participants in this year's Classic would be
heading back to Houston to catch their flights
to connecting flights that would eventually
carry them back to their families. Some with
hopes of next year and others with strange, but
true, tales to relate to their foursome back
home.

There wouldn't be much stretching of the
truth in their stories, as we had left very
little to the imagination. There would be the
believers and the non-believers, but no matter

how the yarns were taken, the legend of The Cut N Shoot Classic would live on yet another year.

I poured myself another scotch and headed for the leaderboard, where I made a mental note of who would be back for Classic XI. Other than myself and with the probable exception of Spook and Kelly, who would most likely be scratching around the countryside with the big boys by then, the guest list would include:

> B.J. Littlejohn of Arizona, with a new skating game.
>
> Bubba Lee of Oklahoma and his sidekick, Jack Daniels.
>
> Lamar Malloy, Jr. of Texas, by way of Dallas.
>
> Jubal Washington of Georgia, along with his Sunday prayer.
>
> Blake Quantrell of California, now no longer a newcomer.
>
> Donald "Pigeon" Towze of Ohio, also no longer a newcomer.
>
> Mikey Lo Bianco of New Jersey, the Hoboken Hero.

I pondered the board even further and counted those who would be MIA from past years:

> Ronnie Hurt of Pennsylvania.
>
> Tinker Brandt of Michigan.
>
> Beau Pritchett of Virginia.
>
> Kenji Lee of Hawaii.
>
> Walt Pearson of Wyoming.
>
> J.T. King of Massachusetts.

With the excused absence of the two soon-to-be professionals, Thumper and I would have to decide how to justly fill their positions and still keep all our states happy. Hell, we might decide to venture out and invite us some foreign players. Nah! We didn't need to start getting whole countries pissed off at us. Besides, Mama might not want to foot the airline bill from Scotland or Japan or wherever.

All this semi-intellectual thinking brought my mind back to old Thumper. He hadn't said a word one to me up on the stage when we were presenting Spook with his trophy. I guessed it was high time I found him and took my expected medicine.

I knew he would be in the clubhouse, so I finished my scotch and headed off in that direction. On the way over, I met B.J., his clubs all bundled up in his flight bag. I made the obvious comment. "You're gonna have plenty of room going home, sharing them to seats with yourself."

He just laughed and thanked me for my usual hospitality. I reminded him not to practice his skating prowess, as it wouldn't be fair to the others. We shook hands, then he headed for his Avis and the hour drive to Houston Intercontinental.

As I approached the clubhouse, I stopped as I heard voices coming from the porch. There was Thumper, carrying on a pleasant conversation with Kelly Dale. I decided to wait until they were through before making my presence known. When I heard Thumper wish him good luck in the future, I stepped up to join them.

We didn't have much to say to each other, me and Kelly, as we had let our golf do all the talking for us earlier. He said he had a plane to catch and didn't want to miss it, especially since he wouldn't be getting back to Farmington until almost two in the morning as it was. I wished him luck also, and as he stepped off the porch, I told him to give my best to his daddy. It must have fallen on deaf ears as he refused to acknowledge it as he rounded the corner and was gone.

Thumper had gone inside and brought out two chairs, so I knew he was at least going to talk to me. He sat himself in the one nearest the door and propped his feet up onto the railing. I joined him, slipping my now aching feet out of my Footjoys for the first time today.

We sat there without speaking as we had done numerous times before, until I finally broke the ice. "Any ideas how we're gonna fill Spook and Kelly's spots next year?" I thought it best to start with something other than my failure to beat Kelly and bring home the trophy.

"One of 'em." As usual, he wasn't going into great detail until he was ready.

"Oh, which one?" I decided to play him at his own game.

"Sure, you don't want a beer first?" In a match-play on words, I was no threat to his game.

"No, but I would be partial to a medium scotch."

With that, he got up slowly from his chair and went inside, returning at leisure with his usual Lone Star and a half-empty bottle of

Cutty. No cup, just the bottle. I took a mean swig and just decided to listen, as he obviously had something he wanted to say, eventually.

"You didn't do too good watching your backside today." I should have expected that, but I wasn't quite ready for it.

"No, I didn't. But I did manage to keep peace in the family." It was a weak answer, but it matched my state of mind at the moment.

"This year anyway." He hesitated and then decided to let it all out at once. "I think we got us a legitimate replacement for Kelly next year. Fella named Chip."

I hoped to myself that Chip was his true given name and not one laid on him for his ability around the greens. I let Thumper continue.

"The kid's a high school senior up in Connecticut, and according to our friend, Kelly, he shoots a mean game of golf."

That was OK by me, since all our invitees hold similar credentials, or they wouldn't be here. I allowed Thumper to keep the floor.

"Kelly said the boy's beaten him at his own game on more than one occasion, so if he meets with your approval, I think we ought to offer him a chance to play your daddy's course, assuming he meets all the qualifications."

I understood by his last comment that he wanted my answer at this very moment. I figured since I hadn't exactly come through for him today, I might as well give him his way, so I offered my approval. "Fine by me. Does Chip have a last name?" I never in my wildest dreams thought that question would have any bearing on the outcome of my decision.

"Dale. Chip Dale."

We didn't talk anymore, just drank. We never got around to discussing Spook's replacement. It really didn't matter now, and we had more than your average amount of time to cross that hazard.

I eventually killed that half-full bottle of Cutty, and as I stumbled my way back across Whipoorwill, I hoped to God that Melanie was there waiting.

T H E   E N D